FORBIDDEN EARTH

Sabina 'Ariana' Anand, a twelve-year-old author born in California, enjoys the creative arts and credits her family for her 'science and fiction genes'. Sabina hopes that her novels will inspire movies some day, movies that will transport us to extraordinary experiences.

FORBIDDEN
EARTH

sabina 'ariana' anand

RUPA

Published by
Rupa Publications India Pvt. Ltd 2013
7/16, Ansari Road, Daryaganj
New Delhi 110002

Sales centres:
Allahabad Bengaluru Chennai
Hyderabad Jaipur Kathmandu
Kolkata Mumbai

ISBN: 978-81-291-2441-8

10 9 8 7 6 5 4 3 2 1

The moral right of the author has been asserted.

Typeset in Dante MT 11.5/15.5

Printed at Repro Knowledgecast Limited, Thane

For Dad,
who always believed.

For Tanvi,
who provided much inspiration.

For Dadi Ma,
who finessed the manuscript.

For Nanu,
who is my marketing champion.

For Mom,
who made it all happen.
&
For my sister

Contents

1. The Landing   1
2. The Creation   4
3. Meeting the Enemy   9
4. In the World of the BCs   13
5. Taking Off (on Earth)   15
6. The Meeting   20
7. The Human and the BC   26
8. Nightmares   30
9. Forbidden Earth   48
10. Decisions   63
11. Settling Down   70
12. Planning in Space   78
13. Preparations   86
14. The Application   93
15. Discovery   102
16. What do I do?   112
17. Trouble in Northern Earth   123
18. Prayer   133
19. Revolution   149
20. Unexpected Results   165

1

The Landing

Macey Johnson and her best friend Leslie Stevens had known each other since kindergarten. They knew everything about each other—from family history to embarrassing moments. The two had grown up to be eighteen together, and were rushing down their main hallway, trying to squeeze through their spaceship door. They had been living in the spaceship their entire life, and had never even seen their home planet. But now, they were finally landing on Earth.

Once Macey and Leslie finally managed to squish themselves through, with a few dozen other people, they were overtaken by astonishment at the beauty of their home planet. As if their arrival had been planned, the spaceship had landed directly in front of a beautiful, rushing waterfall. The water had been painted a slight shade of red because of the sun that was setting over the horizon. They had caught the sunset at the best possible time.

'Unbelievable,' murmured Macey under her breath.

'Gorgeous,' Leslie replied. The two couldn't believe they had been missing out on this in all the eighteen years of their life. As Macey watched the sunset, she couldn't help staring at Leslie as well. Leslie was beautiful already, but the light made her long, blonde locks shimmer. Her blue eyes made Earth's sky look pale and her height was perfect. She wasn't too tall, nor was she too short. She was absolutely flawless.

Macey's focus slowly shifted to her own flat, dark brown hair. She had brown eyes and tan skin. Her head had always only reached Leslie's neck. Macey also had trouble maintaining her weight—she wasn't plump—she just had a hard time staying skinny. Mostly, no one ever seemed to notice her, except for when she smiled.

She had the brightest smile anyone could imagine. It was the kind of smile that could turn someone's day from depressing to absolutely amazing. Macey may not have been the prettiest girl on the spaceship, but her goofy grin evened everything out.

Macey let out a breath she didn't even realize she was holding. As she freed her mind of her thoughts, she opened her eyes to see Leslie snapping her fingers and shouting. 'Hello? Hello? Macey it's time to go in for dinner,' said Leslie. Macey groaned. On the spaceship, with improved technology, they had managed to grow plants in space. They had been eating the same foods for so long.

'What kind of "new" food have they invented for us today?' Macey sighed.

'Actually, this time they've served pretty decent food,' Leslie sighed sarcastically, imitating Macey's expression when it came to talking about dinner on the spaceship. They both chuckled. 'Back to the subject, Macey. Today they're serving lamb lasagna.'

'Where in the world did they find a lamb?' Macey sighed, lying down in the grass.

'Heaven knows,' Leslie replied, imitating a lamb that was being hunted. She scrunched up her nose and started crawling around on her hands and knees. 'Maybe...' Leslie started, but Macey interrupted.

'Let's not think about it!' she said through her laughter. Leslie tossed her head back and stayed silent for a moment, absorbing in all the beauty she could.

'Come on, let's go inside. We can explore Earth later,' she finally said. The two ran inside talking about how immature they could be sometimes, especially for their age.

∾

2

The Creation

It was very easy for Macey and Leslie's minds to wonder as to why they had to spend their life in a spaceship and not be able to live a normal life on Earth. But there was a reason for everything.

As time progressed, technology became more and more complex. New machines were constantly being invented to do things that were thought to be impossible in the past. There was a scientist named Professor David Vega, who lived on Earth a long time back. He was always on the leading edge, coming up with ideas and inventions to do the impossible; no wonder most of them never left his lab. But this time he was almost positive his invention would turn out alright. He was inventing biological computers—BCs for short. He cultured, meticulously picked human cells, modified the biochemistry coding, and created an embryo which would grow into a biological computer adhering to the specifications of the creator.

They looked like humans and talked like humans but they were really computers—living and breathing computers. The biggest difference between BCs and humans was that the BCs worked much harder and stayed focused. They only needed two hours of sleep and they didn't really have emotions. Even if they did, it was for a fleeting moment. Professor David Vega's intention was to program these BCs to be humans' slaves—To do whatever their masters wanted them to do and to work fast and efficiently. But his inventions usually never worked in the real world, at production scale. This was probably the closest he ever got to his goal. They did everything they were programmed to do. But that would soon change.

Most of the BCs worked diligently and accomplished a lot. And then they started getting the idea of freedom. They were smart and they could sense physical labour and hints of slavery. Why were they so good at following instructions and why were their feelings so ephemeral? Little did they know that it was by design. Some thought it was unfair. All this hard labour and little sleep, was it time that they broke free? Maybe even dominate the Earth?

Back in 3060 A.D., Macey and Leslie sat eating their lamb lasagna when they heard a sort of rumbling sound. 'What's that?' questioned Leslie, flipping her blonde hair to look out of the window.

'I hope it's not an earthquake,' replied Macey, not suspecting anything worse. She squinted through the window, trying to see beyond the stains and fingerprints. There was a line of people. 'What? It can't be,' Macey mumbled.

'The BCs! They found us!' Leslie and Macey shouted at the same time. If it hadn't been such a serious situation, they would've laughed. Instead, they went to tell Macey's dad, who was the captain of the spacecraft.

'The BCs are here, Tim!' Leslie exclaimed.

'Yeah, Dad. They're on their way right now,' Macey said, scared that her father might not be buying her unlikely story.

'What? Macey is this one of your tricks again? You're eighteen! I'd think you'd know better than to trick your father. He's getting old!'

'No, Dad—we're serious. Come follow me if you don't believe us,' Macey frowned. Tim knew immediately not to argue. Macey was always such a light-hearted person. If she was serious, it was time to start panicking.

Tim tolled behind Leslie and Macey through the long hallway. Once they arrived back in the dining area, all three of them gathered around the dirty window, hoping it wasn't true. By that time, the BCs were only a few yards away.

'Oh no,' Tim mumbled. 'Oh no, oh no, oh no. Everybody get out! The BCs are here!' A small murmur rippled through all the diners. Immediately, their whispers turned into shouts of terror.

'Remember what they did to our ancestors?' cried one man.

'We can't let that happen to us! Let's move! Come on, let me out!' shouted another. Everybody started rushing through the door. Everyone was scared, yet they all knew fighting back would be better than cowering away. But the BCs were smart too. The only problem was that the generation of humans on the spaceship had never encountered BCs, they had only heard of the stories. On the flip side, there were few BCs who had lived during the time when they had chased off humans from Earth. BCs could live longer than humans, but they died eventually.

The rivals had never met, and there they were charging at each other, neither side knowing what would happen next. All along, Macey was trying to remember all that she had learned about what the BCs had done to humans. Her thoughts made Macey angry, and before she realized it, she had sped up and was running in front of all the other humans. Big mistake. The BCs turned all their focus onto Macey. Muscular arms reached for her torso, and before Macey could think twice...

She had been captured. She started screaming and kicking like a six-year-old as they dragged her away by the arms. All of her friends and family stood there, their jaws dropped.

'Don't just stand there! Help me!' screamed Macey. 'Dad! Leslie! Are you just going to let them take me away like this? What are you doing?' By that time, there were tears streaming down Macey's cheeks. She continued to scream. As Macey's tears dribbled downwards, everyone sped into action.

'Fire your weapons! Don't just stand there! Go get those BCs! That's my daughter up there!' Tim was screaming orders at everybody. However, only ten seconds later, Tim lay sprawled on the floor. The humans were more afraid than ever. *What had happened?* One by one they all toppled over. They could open their eyes but their bodies were unable to move. The few people left standing turned in horror to see the BCs with their snazzy ray guns aimed directly at the humans. To top it off, they had smirks spread wide on their faces. The remaining humans didn't need a ray gun to stay temporarily paralyzed. They soon realized that the BCs were unstoppable. When this occurred to them, the humans who had survived being shot by a BC began to help the paralyzed ones. As soon as they were all up, they all hurried into the spaceship—all except for Leslie and Tim. Leslie, the drama queen, lay on her knees. Her eyes were squinting and her cheeks burned. Out of anger, she pulled grass and roots out of the forest floor as hard as she could and hurled them. Out of sadness, she started screaming and crying. Macey, her best friend since, well, forever, had vanished. She had disappeared with the BCs over the horizon in a hurtling craft.

'Macey! Don't go! Why are you leaving me like this?! Macey!' she screamed, but ran out of air before she could say more. Her stomach was aching from powering the dramatic tears that were strolling down her cheeks onto the soft grass. 'M-Macey!' Leslie's voice faded from a screech to a whisper.

'Leslie, stop being a drama queen. Don't just sit there; come on,' Tim said in a monotone, sprinting into the forest. Tim felt chips of bark cut into his arms as he ran through groves of trees. Leslie hurried after him, calling Macey's name the whole time. Tim, on the other hand, remained silent. Instead of screaming, he followed the path he thought he saw the craft fly.

'She's not gone. She's in this forest. They couldn't have taken her too far yet.' Tim whispered. But with every passing second, Tim started slowing down and running out of breath. It was no surprise that after only a few minutes, the craft was no longer in sight.

was told. After exactly three seconds, Macey opened her eyes again and found herself in front of a giant, marble mansion.

'Wha-how?'

The strongest BC cut her off. 'Don't speak,' he growled.

Macey didn't think she'd ever been more afraid. It wasn't every day you were captured by an alien. Time passed quickly, though, as they walked through the fancy glass door of the mansion, and travelled up the large, shiny elevator. Its walls were constructed of mirrors on all sides, and the golden rods she rested on looked brand new as they reflected the bright lights of the elevator. Eventually, Macey found herself on the twenty-fourth floor of the mansion, seated on a bed as she waited for something to happen. Three burly BCs with shaved heads were staring directly at her. The rest had gone to complete their duties. One BC started to speak clearly and slowly.

'Where did you come from? Why did you come here?'

'Um, well,' Macey said awkwardly. She stopped as her eyes locked with the eyes of the serious looking BC in front of her. 'We all had a motive to see our home planet. The one that our ancestors lived on before you drove them off, you know?' she mumbled with her head down. 'I'm just a kid—well, not really. I'm eighteen, but you know what I mean. Basically, I don't know much.'

'Why not? Aren't you the captain's daughter?' questioned one BC. Although he was being inquisitive, his voice sounded very demanding. More like a statement than a question.

'Well yes, but,' Macey was starting to feel utterly stupid; she had no clue what to say. The BCs seemed as if they knew

3

—∞∞∞—

Meeting the Enemy

Macey had stopped screaming and tried to calm down. *Everything's pointless*, she thought. *My friends, my family, my life...they're all gone. Why did this happen to me? Why me?* She understood she wasn't going to get anywhere by screaming and shouting, so she might as well save her breath.

The smiling BCs started a conversation that was too inaudible for Macey to comprehend. By that time, Macey was really getting freaked out. The craft hovered in the air for another fifteen minutes, and Macey watched the transformation of the thick forest into an urban area. The BCs stopped the craft when they reached a shiny, new looking speed racer. They all got in. Macey wondered why there wasn't a trunk to store things. There were just two scrunched up seats. Why, there wasn't even a steering wheel! All that it included was a small portable GPS. The BCs shoved Macey into the car and started punching in some numbers into the strange looking GPS.

'Close your eyes,' one BC barked at Macey. She did as she

everything. 'I don't know a thing. I was asked to keep a look out for BCs. I was told they were just creatures to look out for. I don't know anything else and I don't care about anything else. I just want to see my family,' Macey blurted. The moment she comprehended what she had said, she slapped her hands over her mouth. She wasn't sure if that was really the answer the BCs were looking for.

'I understand. This is the same thing that happened to us. Our ancestors did not want to be mean. They had no choice,' one BC said. The other two BCs glared at him, as if he was crazy to say such a thing to a human. One started mouthing messages to him, telling him to hush up. Macey pretended to ignore them.

'Why? Why didn't they have a choice?' she asked, facing the BC who had given her a sliver of information.

'According to the President of BCs, humans were a threat to the BCs' existence on Earth,' the talkative BC replied softly. He sounded scared, as if he didn't know what the other two BCs would do to him for spilling so much information.

'Come on, guys. We can't risk too much information,' the strongest BC said. Together, the other two BCs lifted up the BC that had revealed so much of the inside scoop.

'Oh,' Macey's voice trailed off. She was certain that as soon as the three BCs stepped outside, the social BC would be fired immediately. 'How long will I be here?'

'You will only speak when spoken to,' one of the BCs said over his shoulder.

'How did you find us?' Macey asked again, ignoring his comment.

'You don't need to know,' the other one grumbled, annoyed at Macey's persistence.

'Our space protection systems saw your spaceship land. We thought it was an intruder, and apparently we were right. The moment the space controllers made this observation, they dispatched a reaction unit,' the social one of the three mumbled quickly. As soon as those words slipped out, he glanced at his colleagues, suspecting that his days at the Presidential Palace were likely over.

'Why did you bring me out here?' Macey tried again. 'Will you send me back to my family?'

The BC who had revealed so many facts had a sheepish look on his face. He was careful not to say another word as he was pushed outside of Macey's room.

'We'll try to squeeze your side of the story out later,' one of the BCs said. 'Stay here, for now, if you know what's good for you.'

The three of them left Macey sitting there, her eyes shiny and her cheeks red. She didn't know if she would ever see her family again.

❧

4

In the World of the BCs

'*Breaking News! Virus attack may return!*' the man on the broadcast hologram screamed. 'And now a word from reporter Amy Bell.'

Dylan sighed as he switched the hologram off. Dylan was probably the most laid back BC in the history of the BCs, yet even he decided it was time to get up and do something. The entire population of BCs in the world was in a wave of terror. One hundred years ago, there was a giant virus attack in 'Forbidden Earth'. There was a comet that went through the atmosphere (that had no ozone because of pollution), and it brought viruses. Ever since, no BC had lived in Forbidden Earth. You might have flown over it. If you were a brave scientist you might have gone there for a few months. But you would never be able to live there as a BC.

'What happened to you?' asked Dylan's mom, walking into the room.

'The people on the news channel keep blabbering on and

on about this "virus attack",' replied Dylan.

'You know this thing is pretty serious,' said Dylan's mom, switching the hologram on.

'The entire world of BCs is afraid of humans attacking their area of land. They may bring the viruses from Forbidden Earth!' screeched Amy Bell.

'See?' said Dylan. 'The world has gone completely bonkers. We're the ones who attacked the humans and won, aren't we? Besides, what's so bad about humans being in the same world as us?'

'Sweetie, it's hard for me to explain. You'll understand when you get older.'

'I am older, Mom, I'm nineteen! I'm about to move out of this house.'

'Let me restate that. When you have children that you love and care for...you'll understand the importance of safety. Even the slightest bit of danger will make it to your senses,' said Dylan's mom. Dylan didn't understand what was so frightening about wimps living on his planet.

'What dorks,' said Dylan. 'The humans and the rest of the world.'

༄

5

Taking Off (on Earth)

'Wait!' Leslie screamed into the swaying pine trees. Leslie and Tim had given up their search after an hour of desperate cries; they returned to the spaceship. However, Leslie refused to enter the spaceship again. She remained outside, protesting.

The wind was blowing her hair and her skirt swayed and rippled, adding such a dramatic effect. Her fists were clenched and raised so that it looked as though she was punching the air over, and over, but it fought back. Leslie stared into space with her fierce blue eyes: teary, but firm. Behind her, Tim was gawking at how emotional Leslie could be. He opened his mouth to say something, but then thought better of it. He figured he should let Leslie pour her heart out before he mentioned anything. 'We can't just leave! My best friend is gone; lost in the mess of the world of BCs! This–this is…' Leslie couldn't finish. She stopped for a breath. The fists that were punching the air loosened, then tightened more than ever before. 'This is outrageous!' she finally screamed, while throwing plucked, dead grass toward the sky. They landed softly in her shimmery hair. She had been fighting for half an hour, trying to get the spaceship not to take off without Macey.

'I know,' Tim replied softly. 'I know that you miss Macey. We all do.'

'She's somewhere out there. She's not gone! I can feel it in my gut,' sobbed Leslie. Suddenly, she was on her knees, her hands trying to wipe away all her tears.

'I really miss Macey. This is tearing me apart, bit by bit,' Tim explained, staying calm on the outside. 'Ever since her mother died, Macey was all that I had.' He made his eyes squint, to look at the forest around him, as if he would see Macey walking up the hill that the sun had set over. Leslie shook her head slowly, slightly cocking her head so that her curls waved. 'But…I have made a decision.' Tim said, recovering quickly. 'Let's go into my office…we need to talk.'

'Fine,' Leslie finally gave in.

Minutes later, Leslie walked down a dark hallway that only led to one room, and she saw Tim's doorway. A gloomy yellow light reflected across the mahogany floorboards past it. She entered and saw the beautiful chandelier, the one she always adored. Behind it lay the piles of books that had been read over, and over. To bring light into the room, there lay a window at the very back of the room in between two of the bookshelves. The window pane popped outwards a little, and pillows were added on its white surface. It really made quite a comfortable reading spot. In the center of it all lay Tim's desk, papers scattered all over the black, wooden surface.

The drawers were nearly empty, except for a few pens and occasionally a paper-clip, but everything else had its own small space somewhere in Tim's sea of messiness.

Eventually, Leslie found herself twirling around in Tim's brown, worn-out, leather chair. Tears swelled her eyes as she remembered a game she had made up on this very chair a few years ago with Macey. This chair had always been one of Macey's favourites: the way it was worn out, but still so much fun to play with.

They were little at the time, maybe six or seven, when they made up a game called 'The Dare Chair'. Leslie would sit down in the chair, and Macey would give her a small dare (such as 'stick all your limbs out' or 'hang upside down'). Then, Macey would twirl the chair around as fast as she could, while Leslie tried to stay seated on the chair, performing the dare that Macey had dared her to. Once, when Macey dared Leslie to stand on her head while twirling around, Leslie fell down and broke her wrist.

Leslie rubbed her wrist and felt the bones that had once broken, but were now healed, thanks to Macey's uncle, Dr Mike. Leslie imagined how that kind face would frown when Dr Mike found out his niece was missing.

Other than that, Macey and Leslie had so much fun playing the 'The Dare Chair'. Leslie figured that Tim remembered the game too, the way his expression changed after seeing Leslie twirling around in it.

'That seat,' breathed Tim, rubbing his hands together in a nervous way, and staring at his feet. As always, his large biceps flexed when he moved his arm. He pulled over a small, wooden chair and plopped himself in front of Leslie. He and Leslie exchanged nervous glances as they braced themselves for whatever was going to happen next.

'It reminds me of Macey,' Leslie and Tim said at the same time.

'That also reminds me of what I needed to talk to you about. I miss Macey as much as you do, if not more. The fact is I'm the captain of this spacecraft. As captain, I have very important decisions to make, you know that, right?' Tim asked. Leslie nodded. 'I also have dozens of lives to take care of. After much thinking, I've realized that it is my responsibility to make sure our crew stays safe. My duty as a captain comes before my duty as a dad. I'm afraid we have to say goodbye.' Leslie sucked in a breath, fighting the strong urge to break out in tears.

'Tim, I know that I'm a huge drama queen. On a regular basis, I would kick, scream, and protest. But I understand. I don't agree with you, necessarily, but I do understand. Go ahead. I trust you.'

Tim sighed. 'You do understand that I still love Macey with all my heart; and this is the hardest decision I've ever made, right?' Leslie nodded silently.

'Tim, don't worry about me. I respect your choices. After all, you are Macey's father. I have faith in your decision,' Leslie assured him.

'Great. Then if you'll excuse me, I have to get to the control room.' As soon as Tim said those words, Leslie couldn't hold it in any longer. She knew that Tim was doing the right thing, but everything was just too much to handle.

Leslie ran to her room and flopped on her bed, sobbing her eyes out. She stayed there for only half an hour before feeling the spaceship rumble under her feet. That was it. The spaceship was taking off. She would never see her dearest Macey again.

6

―⊶⊷―

The Meeting

I'm sure you remember Dylan. Although Dylan was a BC, he didn't match up to the standards of a typical BC.

Dylan was almost lazy, which was atypical of a BC. His floppy brown hair looked blonde in the light, and brushed against his eyes occasionally. His amber eyes glistened in the light. His smile however, was the best part. His perfect, straight white teeth revealed how careful he was when he went for his annual check-up at the dentist. The smooth skin around his eyes slightly crinkled when he even showed the slightest bit of a half-hearted smile. Macey and Dylan would've been really great friends.

'No, Mom. For the thousandth time I do not know where your hoop earrings are!'

'Dylan, honey. I didn't ask about my hoop earrings. I asked you if you wanted something to drink before we left for maybe the biggest night of your life! You're meeting the girl—the human—who was captured when some BCs attacked their shuttle. Don't you think that's...well...something?'

'No Mom, I don't want something to drink,' Dylan blankly replied while staring off in the direction of the hologram. Not *at* the hologram. But right through it...as if it wasn't there. Dylan's mom, April, sighed dramatically. Her arms started to flail as if she was an actress in a movie posing as a girl praying to the heavens for a miraculous event that would never happen.

'Dylan, honey...'

'Just stop! Okay? I don't want to meet some random girl they took off the other side of the world! I don't care what she thinks of me! Why would you care what she thinks of me? It's my life and I will live it the way I want to...,' Dylan racked his brain for something more to hurt his mom's feelings. He hated it when she babied him like this. Thankfully, he knew how to annoy her, which is exactly what he did.

'All right, Mr Know-it-all. Next time you try taking care of yourself. I don't see how you can do that, being the *lazy* BC you are.'

Now it was Dylan's feelings that would be hurt—no matter how much he knew that the statement was true. His eyes flickered around the room as if they were broken flashlights. Slowly, he began observing everything from his favourite dusty, blue rug on the living room floor to the tapestry of horses and riders that he had bought during his visit to LeRoyale Earth. He glanced at his medals that he had won at school for getting the best grades in school...though it was mostly because of his Mom's 'help' in homework. Finally he looked at his mother's soft, light brown hair that waved only a little past her shoulders. At that moment, her hair was tied in a loose bun that bobbed whenever she walked. Dylan brought his eyes lower and stared into her large, gorgeous green-blue eyes that showed how upset she was. His gaze continued down her sea-green strapless dress that wrapped tightly around her lean, hourglass-figure. April looked a bit like a model...okay, *a lot* like a model. Her beauty continued all the way down to her toes, which were painted a shiny shade of candy-apple-red. Painted on top were teeny-tiny roses with alternating pink and white petals. Dylan knew that they would still show under her open-toed high-heeled shoes.

But before his mother could speak, the phone blared through the house.

'Call from Melanie!' screeched the caller ID robot. April's glare stayed on Dylan as she backed off the sofa and toward the phone. She left a warm dent where she had previously been sitting, and Dylan knew that many people would pay to sit in that exact spot as April Brown, 'the pretty girl who hadn't been noticed by the directors yet'.

'Hey, Melanie!' her voice sweetened as she gushed into the phone. Dylan could faintly hear Melanie's reply.

'Hi, April,' Melanie said with much less excitement. She sounded as if she was utterly bored with April's hyper attitude. Melanie was April's age and April's friend, but she had always loved Dylan like a son. Melanie hesitated before talking, and as usual, her voice turned sickly-sweet as she asked about Dylan. 'Is Dylan home? I...um...was wondering if you would bring him over for some cookies later. Oh, and yourself!' Melanie hurried to add.

April shook her head in disbelief. 'I'm sorry, but we are off to the most important night of our lives. Even though Dylan refuses to believe it. Okay, good-bye now!' She hung up the phone before Melanie had a chance to say bye.

April returned to her angry mode with Dylan. 'Dylan, stay where you are!' she snapped. Dylan was amazed. He was inching away from the sofa, cautious in order to be as slow as a snail. His blank stare continued until he found his voice again.

'What are you, a super-spy?' he asked.

'No,' she said, while setting herself next to Dylan once again. Dylan started to seriously consider how much cash he would make if he sold the couch.

April continued without a bat of an eye. 'I'm a normal BC and you're not. Now let's go.'

Since BCs were really fast, they walked or ran to most places. So as Dylan sprinted down the sidewalk, yards in front of April, his mind began to wonder as to why April would dress so prettily just to see a girl at a human exhibit in a history museum.

It later occurred to Dylan, though, that April wasn't the only one. Everybody was coming dressed for what seemed like a prom because, just like April, they believed that it would be the biggest night of their lives.

As if they have one, Dylan joked silently, to himself.

Who could blame them? It was truly a once in a lifetime event.

As Dylan caught sight of the history museum—it was

kind of hard to miss it, with the big HISTORY MUSEUM sign—he started to slow down. He observed the huge, bold letters painted onto the wooden sign that hung from two iron chains. He noticed the rust that had started to form near the ends of the chains. The place was like one of those schools or libraries that were new, but had the old feel. Such as buildings that had brick walls and white pillars.

But walking into the museum was a whole different story. Dylan looked down as he forced himself to put one foot in front of the other. The sun had set around half an hour ago, and his scruffy shoes were lit by the streetlights and all the gleaming holiday lights set up on the history museum. Once he looked up, he saw something that took his breath away.

The small cheap lamps that had been hanging on the ceiling ever since he was born had been replaced with chandeliers that cast a bright glow on the polished, new tile floor. Men and women of all sizes flooded the room. The men were all just a swirl of black and white tuxes, but the women on the other hand looked like a kaleidoscope of bright dresses. Dylan's gaze shifted to his own torn, baggy jeans. He didn't even remember the last time he had washed them. They were rough to the touch, as well as his t-shirt. April had asked him to change into a 'proper, formal shirt or at least a polo'. His shirt was one that he wore when he was about sixteen, but it was still too big for him. It read *I'm not short, I'm fun size.* Although he wasn't short—or fun size. He was really tall for his age. While Dylan sat thinking, a large, animated voice blared through the loud bullhorn. 'I know what you have all gathered here for tonight,' the host shouted. 'And you will not leave this museum disappointed!' he bellowed. Typical host talk. 'Please welcome...' *Please quiet down*, Dylan thought.

The crowd started murmuring, then cheering. 'The human!' shouted a man.

'An actual human!' shouted another.

'No way,' the sarcastic, plump woman sighed next to him. Dylan couldn't bear the excitement. After about five minutes, his head started throbbing. *I better go outside for a fresh breath of air. But first, I should find April.* However, after circling his table only once, Dylan decided his headache was too severe and he couldn't stay inside any longer. By the time he put one foot in front of the other and made it outside of the museum, Dylan's feet were sweating and his knees felt wobbly. Soon enough, his jelly-like knees buckled and he fell onto the floor, unconscious.

7

The Human and the BC

'Wake up sleepyhead...' Dylan awoke to the sound of a sweet sing-song voice.

'W-Where am I?' Dylan asked, still dazed from his meltdown.

'In front of my "exhibit",' Macey laughed. That was when Dylan saw Macey's smile. The smile that set him off wondering where would he ever find a more flawless girl. The human reached in and brushed some hair away from his eyes, making the image of her white teeth even clearer.

'You know you can come over for lunch or something— somewhere—sometime,' Dylan stopped himself realising how lame he sounded. But if Macey noticed she didn't show it at all.

'I would love that! That is, if these BC's ever let me go. No offense,' Macey could have punched herself for sounding so self-centred.

She hoped this boy wasn't like the other BCs who kept her captive like some sort of alien. Deep inside, she had a feeling this boy was nothing like that. This boy appeared special. Someone who actually saw her as the real her, and not what she was judged by, or where she was from. She decided she liked this guy. A whole lot. 'What's your name?'

'Dylan. Don't bother telling me your name—I already know—you being the human and all.' *Ugh. Pull yourself together.*

'Whatever. I have to go now. The BCs back at the mansion just paged me telling me it's time to head back. I enjoyed talking to you. I'll find a way to contact you about your invitation, Dylan. Bye!'

'Good-bye...' Dylan said dreamily, wondering if and when he would ever see his Macey again.

'Oh, it was great!' Dylan replied to April's question on how the night was.

'Ha! I told you so! I knew you would love it! The food, the excitement, the human! Oh my gosh, I can't imagine a better night!'

'Gosh, Mom, trust me on this one. Neither can I,' Dylan said with a smile. He brushed the hair from his forehead just the way Macey did to him. *Macey* he thought. *What a sweet, innocent sounding name.* Dylan shook his head in disbelief as he murmured under his breath.

'What's wrong, sugar?' asked April, looking beautiful as always. Her shimmering, topaz eyes showed the concern that she felt.

'I just don't get it, Mom. What's the point of capturing

these humans? What did they ever do to us? I know they made us their slaves a *long* time ago, but they did create us for that purpose. Without them, we wouldn't be here. And here we are treating them like dirt. They deserve better. Especially Macey.' Dylan repeated her name slowly, as if it had to be said perfectly.

But what was the point? He knew April would never get it. She was just like all the other BCs. She wasn't there to witness the amazing sensations Macey could gift you in a single smile. No other BC would ever know. That's when Dylan decided to rescue Macey. He didn't know how he would do it, but he would figure the mess out. There was no way he was treating her like anything other than who she was.

Macey couldn't believe a week had passed by and nobody had come to rescue her. She was starting to really think that there was no chance of her ever getting back to her family. Every Wednesday, her dad, Leslie, and she had family fun night, and she wondered if Tim and Leslie had continued their tradition without her. Her hope was that they hadn't. Her mind was filled with swirling thoughts and she just couldn't handle it. *How will I contact Dylan? Was he serious? Will my family ever come to save me? When will I see Leslie again? Why did this happen to me? What's wrong with my life!?* As this blizzard whirred through her head, her short, soft hair fell from behind her ear and made a dark curtain that separated her from the rest of the cruel world. Tears began to flow from her eyes.

It was then that she saw a tiny piece of yellow paper peeking out from the closet door. She went over to see what it was. As she unfolded the tiny piece of paper, it revealed a gigantic map that showed all of the four, evenly divided sections of Earth: Northern Earth (Where she was), LeRoyale Earth (to the south of Northern Earth), Mahay Earth (to the east of Northern Earth), and Forbidden Earth (origin of the malignant virus, and abandoned by BCs). Forbidden Earth seemed like it was where her spaceship was located, judged by the news, the BCs' talk, and the surroundings from where she had landed. Apparently, the beautiful place where their spaceship left its marks was likely to be filled with viruses that BCs could be infected by, because of their lack of immunity. 'Jackpot,' Macey said as her tears stopped running down her skin. 'Now all I have to do is find the thing that transported me here and go back to Forbidden Earth!' Which was, of course, easier said than done.

8

Nightmares

'Tim, I miss Macey,' wailed Leslie. She tossed her head back. Secretly, Leslie felt that Tim had made a huge mistake. She wanted to head back to Earth. But of course, she never mentioned this to Tim.

'It's difficult Leslie. I miss her too. But you know how it is: my job's a major priority.' Leslie felt like a rock just landed in her stomach, making it sink as far as it could go. It was impossible for her to speak. Finally, she said what was on her mind.

'Well, maybe your job as a dad is equally as important. In my opinion, we need to focus on Macey.' Tim didn't listen to her. He dismissed Leslie quickly, convinced she was still living in her past. But deep down, way inside, Tim wished Leslie was right.

That night, Leslie didn't sleep well. She had happy dreams that ended in nightmares. She had a vision of Macey and herself when they were younger and were playing dress-up on the spaceship. She heard Macey's musical voice and tinkling laugh, but suddenly, she was in the arms of a kidnapper, screaming and yelling as she was dragged away. 'No!' Leslie screamed in her sleep. 'No, no, no!' She shot up like a bullet, and saw Tim by her side trying to comfort her.

'It was just a dream, just a dream,' he was saying, while holding her and rubbing her head. But Leslie knew not to believe him. It was all reality. Every single bit of it.

When Dylan woke up, he was feeling groggy and cloudy. The usual two hour sleep that he got as a BC had reduced down to two minutes. He had stayed up almost the whole two hours thinking about Macey and his dangerous plan to go out and rescue her, as if it really was going to happen. Even if he didn't know the first step, Dylan would go outside and start looking for anything that would inspire him. It was 2:00 a.m., and the streets were crowded with BCs who had completed their two hours of sleep. Restaurants, shooting ranges, theaters, you name it. Everything was so full. He roamed down the streets until he approached the President's mansion. Suddenly, an imaginary light bulb flickered over Dylan's head. How could he be so dumb? Of course Macey was in there! After all, it was the President's idea to capture her. *It's all smooth sailing from here,* he thought. *Let's do this thing.*

'I'm here to visit, I swear! I was at the convention in the history museum, but I...uh... fell asleep halfway through.' Dylan pleaded, unsuccessfully. The security guard in front of the Presidential Palace did not seem convinced. 'If you don't believe me, just call up her room and ask.'

'She's sleeping, smart one,' he snarled sarcastically. 'Nobody can be as perfect as you think you are. You can't expect me to make an exception for you. It's your fault. You should have stayed up.' An annoyed look covered the security guard's face.

'Just call up her room. She's expecting me. I cross my heart. If she's sleeping, I'll leave.' Dylan crossed his fingers behind his back, hoping the guard couldn't hear the lie that edged his voice.

'Alright.' The security guard nodded his head in approval. 'But if the human's asleep, you're the one to blame.' *As if you care what happens to her.* Dylan thought. *Selfish beast.*

'Don't be scared, I'm not like the others,' Dylan flashed his brilliant smile at Macey. The mysterious feeling in the air either meant Macey was dreaming, or she was a complete lunatic. But she was certain it was the first option. Or at least she hoped so. 'Come on, I won't harm you,' said Dylan. But something in his tone told her that he would. She stepped closer anyway. Suddenly Dylan grasped her in his grip of steel and dragged her into the woods. She squirmed and squabbled, unable to break free.

'Let. Me. Go!' she screamed and jolted up in bed, her

head swirling with sudden thoughts and fears. 'No,' she told herself. 'Dylan is not a monster. He is not like the others. He cares. He loves.' She continued to think about Dylan's smile, his hair, personality, and uniqueness. She looked at the clock once she had calmed down to find that it was 2:30 a.m. She wasn't sleepy at all, so she forced her legs—which had fallen asleep—to pull over her bedside and onto the plush cream carpet beneath her. She stared at the twin bed opposite from her own and traced the checkered pattern of the bed sheets.

While recalling the map she found—that was now safely stored in the secret compartment she discovered in her dresser—she thought about how she would break out of the heavily protected mansion she was being held captive in. There was no way.

Macey got up to open her heavy floral curtains that guarded her grand window to reveal the most lit up night sky she had ever seen. Lights shone from buildings and streetlights were illuminated completely. Even if it was 2:30 a.m., it could easily have passed as 7:00 p.m. At least according to the holographic movies that Macey had watched in her spaceship while growing up. Even the restaurants were full of BCs, and spotlights could be seen dancing in front of the one and only Northern Theatre of the Youth (NTY for short). *Of course,* Macey thought. *BCs rarely have to sleep.* Macey's head was still swirling and she felt like barfing. As if somebody had taken her, rolled her into a ball, cramped her in a tiny bottle, and then taken her out the next day. Her lungs were working fine, but she still gasped for air.

Macey made her way to the bathroom that neighboured her enormous bedroom and washed her face with water so cold, it felt like ice. The water dripped from her eyelashes making the droplets look like tears she had never cried. On the bright side, it helped her think straight.

The icy tiles beneath her feet brought chills up Macey's spine, and she decided it would be better to do this in her bedroom rather than inside the bathroom.

Once back in her posh room, Macey returned to her window. *I've never seen anything like it.* She marveled. *This place is so bright, so well-guarded, that a whole group of thieves couldn't break into the smallest of houses here.* Not that there were any small houses in such a rich community. The streets were just clustered with mansion after mansion. Macey came to realize she didn't even know whose home she was staying in and that she hadn't found time to explore the place that could be her dwelling for—well heaven knows how long.

She dropped her eyes and rested her gaze upon the gate that chaperoned all the activity that took place in front of this palace. Who went in, who went out, even what somebody was doing inside that very minute. How could she possibly be happy in a place like this? But then the answer struck her. Dylan. Her happiness. It was all in his hands. *But how will I find him, if they don't even let me out of this hallway?* She inquired. It didn't make sense. Suddenly, the old fashioned phone that rested on her bedside table blared, echoing the annoying sound off the walls and waking her up from her trance. Macey scrambled over the bed, in a hurry to answer before the call went to voice mail. *Who could be calling me at this time?* The only thing keeping her from ending the call was the slither of hope that the person on the other end of the line was Dylan.

'Hello?' she answered breathlessly, and a bit too quickly.

'Hello? Human?' A gruff voice answered. *The security guard.* Macey thought. *Why would he be calling me?*

'I have a name you know,' Macey said, annoyed. She could hear some tugging and chaos going on from the other end and suddenly she was worried. What if somebody here was to take her somewhere more horrible than where she already was? (Even though her place was luxurious, it was treacherous as well.) But then she thought of the bright side. What if somebody was there to take her home? To visit her? What if it was Dylan?

'Are you expecting a young lad to visit you by the name of...' there was some murmuring on the other end. 'Dylan Brown?'

'Yes!' she croaked desperately. 'Send him up immediately.' The guard sounded a little surprised on the other end, and Macey could just see Dylan smirking smugly.

'Told you so,' she heard his voice say. Instantly, Macey was launched into a fantastic daydream of what Dylan could be there for.

The entire elevator ride, Dylan was pondering over what he would say to Macey. What if she'd rather stay prisoner than run away with a stupid guy like himself? What if he was too late and Macey had already fallen in love with someone else? *What if...? What if...?*

Ding! 'Twenty-fourth floor,' said the operator in its robotic, repetitive voice. Dylan stepped out and took a huge breath. His heart was thudding. This was his chance to make a good impression, and he couldn't help but think about all the ways it could go wrong.

'Room six, room six,' he repeated to himself. Ah, there it was. His hand reached out to touch the door knob, and he took another deep breath as he pushed the soundless door open. Macey was at the window, studying something that looked like a huge piece of paper. He snuck up behind her, careful not to make any sound. As his feet grew closer, Macey didn't move an inch. After a few moments, Dylan began to grow impatient. *Keep breathing. Deep breaths,* he told himself. The fears in his mind had started to fade, but butterflies fluttered in their place. Finally, Dylan mustered enough courage to start talking. But as soon as he inhaled, Macey stiffened. Slowly and cautiously, she angled her head at a strange position as if not to reveal anything behind her. 'Hey,' Dylan said sheepishly.

Macey gasped with happiness as she quickly hid the piece of paper she was studying. 'Dylan!' she whispered as she threw her hands around his neck. Her cold fingers felt icy and fresh next to his burning skin. Hesitantly, he awkwardly moved his arms around to touch her back. 'I thought I'd never see you again. I thought you were joking. I never expected you to make it!' she exclaimed. Her sudden change of expression showed how shocked she was at her slip of words. Suddenly her face grew dark and her eyes turned cloudy. She froze and narrowed her eyes until they were tiny slits. 'You're not here as a spy right?' she inquired.

'No.'

'A news reporter?'

'No.' Macey said the next one hesitantly as if she was planning the words in a way that wouldn't offend Dylan.

'A criminal?'

'For heaven's sake, no, Macey! I'm here because I'm not a liar, or a cheater. I keep my promises. I'm here to see you,' Dylan smiled. His voice turned into a hushed whisper. 'More importantly, I'm here to rescue you,' he said, leaning closer so nobody could hear them. Then he backed up, a smug look on his face as he waited for Macey to register what he just said.

'Dylan. I knew you weren't like the others. Thank you,' she whispered excitedly. 'What's the plan?' she asked.

'That's exactly what we need to figure out.'

'You mean you don't have a plan?' she gasped. Her fingers clenched into fists and her face turned red. 'Dylan! How could you do this to yourself?' she fumed. Macey expected Dylan to get mad about her mood change. After all, he was risking his safety to save her. But then again, BCs didn't have complex feelings other than a minor, simple sense of focused attraction that one may call love.

'Keep calm, Macey. It's alright. The worst that can happen is that we don't get out this time, and if so, I will visit again. Okay?' Macey soundlessly nodded her head in agreement, calming herself down.

'Thanks Dylan. For what you are doing,' she whispered. Her hand went over to touch his. Shocked by this new action, Dylan wove his fingers through hers. *Be human.* He told himself.

∾

We're holding hands! Macey marveled. That was a step. 'So...' she said, trying to break the awkward silence. 'Any ideas for the rescue mission?'

'Uh...nah,' he said, pushing Macey's hand away with firm fingers. Macey's face fell. Dylan ignored her sudden change. 'Well,' he continued. 'Whatever we do, I think it'll be best if we drive the guard away instead of trying to sneak out while he's watching. The guy's got eyes like a hawk.'

'Yep,' agreed Macey, her face turning an apparent shade of pink. Suddenly, they heard heavy footsteps thumping up the wooden hall. Macey's red face immediately turned a pale shade, and she looked like she was going to pass out.

'Macey. Macey! It's okay, everybody knows I'm here.' Dylan tried to calm her.

'Hide Dylan. Hide in the best spot you can find,' she whispered.

'But why?'

'Just do it! Right now!' she said more frantically as the door knob started to turn. Quickly and gracefully, Dylan dove underneath the bed. Macey knew Dylan could do better. She shot a glare that was so severe in the direction of the bed; Dylan got the butterflies all over again. He closed his eyes and huddled into a ball, shutting his ears out as if that would help him stay still. The door creaked open, and Macey immediately relaxed.

'It's only you,' Macey breathed, as if the invisible force squeezing her lungs had finally released her. 'Hey, Emma.' Macey glanced at Dylan, who was now slowly peeking at the interesting woman before him. *Can I come out now?* He mouthed, and saw Macey faintly nod in his direction.

'Who's your little friend?' a tough, but sweet voice asked. It was obvious to Dylan that the woman in front of him was Emma. Macey opened her mouth to answer, but shut it immediately when she saw Dylan was planning on answering for himself.

'My name's Dylan,' he said, taking his hand out to shake hers. Dylan's rough, angular hand looked like a monster's compared to Emma's soft, delicate one. The action made Macey uncomfortable, even though Emma was old enough to be Dylan's mom. Emma, being the smart woman that she was, seemed to notice this.

'You picked a keeper,' she laughed. Her laugh was hearty, and made others want to chorus along with her. Macey flushed for the second time since Dylan came.

'It's not like that,' Macey managed, and turned her head to see Dylan was laughing along too. She turned her head back towards Emma to study her laughing complexion. Her well-built muscles moved back and forth, and her curved stomach tucked in. The soft, reddish-brown hair that covered her head was tied back into a high, tight ponytail that reached her mid-back. Macey noticed for the first time that Emma's face was perfect in almost every way, and her mischievous, dark eyes always reflected the happiness she was feeling. Emma was a warm-hearted BC, and BCs like her were rare on Earth.

Macey felt instantly jealous, but she had to think on the bright side. *That's why I like her so much,* Macey thought, momentarily forgetting her humiliation. 'Emma, I'm so glad you're here! Dylan and I needed your help.'

'What do you need, kiddo?' she said, her eyes still laughing. She stopped immediately when she saw Macey's face. 'What's wrong?'

'I want to run away. Escape with you and Dylan. See my family!' Macey whined, with a pleading and hopeful expression. Emma looked shocked, but after a few seconds, her expression softened. Her stiffened arms went over to touch Macey's head. She joined Macey on the well decorated bed.

Emma threw her arm over Macey's left shoulder and let Macey rest her head on her own. 'Don't worry, squirt. I won't let you down. You know me. Have I ever let you down?' Macey thought about it. There was never a time when she even needed Emma's help. How could she have let her down?

'No, I guess,' Macey mumbled, still looking at the floor.

'Exactly. I'll help you escape. On one condition—I won't go with you on your voyage to find your family,' she proclaimed, slowly, and carefully.

'Why not?' Macey demanded.

'What would you think if suddenly one of your top employees and prisoner went missing on the same day? Would it not be obvious?'

'I'm not cruel enough to keep a prisoner,' Macey challenged. Emma rolled her eyes.

She paused to take something out of her pocket. A set of keys. Macey completely forgot Emma worked here. She had a simple job, as well as a quick brain. Her job was to overlook all the historical records and make laws that would benefit the future. 'There's an advantage to working here, you know. I feel bad doing this, but I would feel worse if I let you rot here

like this. Come on, let's get this over with.' Emma walked out
the door in one, graceful movement. Macey and Dylan stood
gawking behind her.

They found their way behind Emma and followed closely
behind, their shoulders almost touching. Macey was careful
not to push it too far. She took one second to steal a glance
at Dylan, but by the time she turned her head back, Emma
had disappeared from sight completely.

'W-Where did she go?' Macey questioned, eyeing the hole
in the perfect floorboards.

'Just down that hole,' Dylan said with mock irritation.
Soon, Dylan had disappeared from sight as well. 'Come on!'
he yelled. 'It's a small drop!'

'Easy for you to say! You're a BC!'

Dylan wasn't bothered by this at all, as Macey had expected
him to be. Instead, he hollered again. 'Come on, we're here
to catch you if you fall.' His voice echoed endlessly through
the hallway Macey assumed was down there. She trembled
with fear as she swung one leg over the edge. Slowly, she
dragged her other leg over as well. Soon, she was hanging by
her fingertips, and her shaking gave her away. Macey didn't
have time to scream, because she found herself immediately
in Emma's soft arms. For a second, Macey was glad Emma's
arms cradled her instead of Dylan's tough limbs. She let go
of that thought quickly.

'Nice catch,' Dylan smirked.

'Shut it,' Macey said as she playfully punched Dylan's arm.
Emma put Macey back on her feet, and started laughing with
them.

Macey was right; there was a hallway that had been paved under their feet. It was dimly lit, and the limited light danced around the floor. 'Come on,' Emma teased. 'We have to get there today, not tomorrow.'

They soon reached a staircase that spiraled down so far, Macey couldn't see the end of it. *Step aerobics, don't fail me now,* she thought. As she continued down the stairs, she began to slow down. As expected, she was the only one out of her party who did so. Emma and Dylan continued as if they could go on forever.

'Guys,' she gasped. 'A little help?' Dylan came rushing to her side and wove one arm under her legs, and the other at the base of Macey's neck. He lifted her easily, as if she were a feather, and carried her down the flight of stairs. Even then, he didn't slow down. At the end of the stairs, Dylan placed Macey back on her feet. She sauntered along, as if she was still limp. Nobody commented. In fact, they slowed down their pace until she wasn't falling too far behind.

Finally, Emma stopped at a small, narrow door that read *Authorized Personnel Only. Do not enter.* 'Perfect,' Emma smiled, rolling the 'r'.

'Where does this lead?' Macey said flatly. The air in the hallway was starting to smell damp and musty.

'The basement!' Emma exclaimed, as the old door creaked open, its hinges squeaking three octaves higher than expected. Her hand flew to her mouth in the blink of an eye. 'Sorry!' she whispered. 'I'll keep it down!' Emma hopped around the door frame, eager to have Dylan and Macey rush in quickly.

'And...what exactly are we in the basement for?' Macey

asked. The place was a mess. Boxes were piled up in corners, and were jutting out at odd angles. Unwanted, old furniture lay all around, indulged in seas of cobwebs and dust. Water dripped from pipes and created slippery, mucky puddles on the floor. The ground was dirty, and Macey was certain she could hear rats scurrying along the cement floor. She wondered how such a dirty place could be attached to the beautiful mansion that lay above their heads.

'You ask too many questions,' Emma said, clearly annoyed. 'I know what I'm doing.' Macey didn't say another word as she followed Emma to the other end of the basement—just an occasional sigh or two. Dylan, on the other hand didn't stop blabbering. He rambled on about his family (April did he say?), his hatred for work, his school, his friends, and the day he met Macey (the only part Macey bothered to pay attention to). Macey clung mostly to Emma, as if to show she wasn't paying attention to Dylan. Emma's stocky build allowed enough space between Macey and Dylan to feel comfortable.

'Here we are,' Emma interrupted. 'Sorry for stealing the spotlight, Dylan,' she smiled sarcastically. Dylan glared back. Macey looked around for a moment. She saw nothing but a bare, cement wall covered with spiders and dust. In fact, the air was starting to smell even more malodorous.

'But I...I don't see anything,' Macey mused. Her shoulders loosened at the joke, and she was instantly reminded of Leslie. *Stop it. Stop it right now. Don't be a baby.* She took a deep breath and tried to relax. 'Emma, what is this?'

Emma chuckled, clearly amused. 'See that sewage drain right over there?' she pointed under their feet. Her focus was fixed on a large, round flap that looked fixed into the solid ground. Macey bent over and attempted to pull the flap open, but it was stuck.

'Can't...get....it...open!' she gasped, finally letting go. She could've been pushing against a brick wall for all the progress she was making. Her hands fell to her knees, and she tucked her head, catching her breath. 'You expect that to open?' she shook her head. Dylan tried next. He walked towards the sewage drain and lifted it with ease.

'Next time you let the BCs handle it,' he said calmly. Macey made a face and stuck out her tongue. She imitated his sentence on a higher pitch. All Dylan did was chuckle softly. *How can I stay mad at him?* Macey scolded herself.

Emma interrupted her thoughts with a simple 'Are you coming or what?' Emma was standing up, her feet rested beneath the opened flap (which was clearly a disguise). They were resting on a step that led down a series of multiple, short staircases. Her hands weren't anywhere close to the dirty basement ground; they rested underneath her chin, while her elbows took the weight of her face. Gracefully, in dance-like movements, Emma popped her head under the hole, and led the way down the first staircase. Dylan did the same.

Macey, however, had a bit of a struggle. 'Ew, ew, ew!' she muttered all the time. 'You guys are disgusting!' When she got the chance to look at her hands again, they were covered in greenish-brown muck. 'Gross!' she turned her head in disgust, as she peeled the stuff off her hands. Somehow, Dylan and Emma had managed to keep their hands clean. Macey felt a pang of jealousy echo through her stomach. 'You guys have to act all perfect every day. Doesn't it annoy you?' she snarled. Reminded of their cause to come here in the first place, Macey shut up immediately.

The three of them walked down the dirt paved hall, all the while the lighting dimming more and more. In fact, it was almost pitch black. Macey was worried about her safety, but Dylan....

'How long ago was this built? What was it built for? Why isn't it used today?' He chattered on and on and on. Emma kept her cool, and answered the questions sedately.

Apparently the hallway was made for an emergency exit in case of a natural disaster, or when the President was just elected, just to escape the paparazzi. Of course, that didn't work out very well. It wasn't being used at the moment because there had been no natural disasters lately—other than the virus attack in Forbidden Earth, where no BC dwelled—and the President had no need to escape because he was elected three years ago. The paparazzi had started cooling down.

At the end of the hallway, was yet another door. Macey had walked through so many doors and jumped through so many holes by now, she wouldn't care if she never did it again.

'Finally,' Emma sighed with pleasure. 'Here you are, squirt. I promise I'll visit. You'll be in Forbidden Earth, right?' she said, leaning over to wrap her strong arms around Macey's feeble neck.

'Right,' Macey agreed, patting the map that was buried in her pocket.

'I'll miss you, kiddo,' she smiled. Macey was certain Emma would cry if she was human. 'And you're friend Mr Chatterbox over there too,' she gestured towards Dylan, who was staring at the door, waiting to be noticed. He seemed surprised at the way he was noted.

'Nice knowing you Emma,' he said in a monotone, reaching out to shake her hand. 'Now if you don't mind, will you let me and Macey out of the door?'

'Of course,' she said, shocked at the sudden change of mood. She brought out her keys. They dangled from her fingers, echoing a chiming sound through the hall. After fiddling with the keys for a second, Emma's hand touched the doorknob and the door opened inaudibly. Macey tried to focus on what would be waiting for her right outside the door. Would there be another hole to jump through? A fence to climb? Just the open air?

Macey was shaking with fear, anxiety, sadness, and excitement all at the same time. Her questions were answered when the door opened and Macey smelt the first fresh air she'd felt on her face in months. 'Ahh,' she gasped. 'Breathable air!' she marveled, taking in as much of it in as she could at once. But before she progressed any further, Macey turned around to see Emma, darling Emma, who would have to return to her work without a friend.

'Oh, Emma! I'll miss you dearly!' she said flying over to jump into her stiff arms. It was a stupid reaction. It was also the best she could do. 'How will you find me? Forbidden Earth is so big! A-And you could fall sick! With the virus!'

'Don't worry about me kid,' she whispered, kissing Macey's head like a mother. She had truly loved Macey like a daughter, and Macey bet Emma would love Tim and Leslie. 'I stuck a tracker in your back pocket.' She smiled at her joke and sniffled at the same time.

'I'll miss you mo...Emma,' she replied as coolly as she could. Then she waved goodbye, and walked out onto the busy streets of Northern Earth.

∾

9

Forbidden Earth

'Macey,' said Dylan, his velvety smooth voice wrapped around Macey like a too-tight blanket. For a second Macey was in heaven, despite the fact Leslie and Tim were missing.

'Yes?' she asked dreamily. Her hands and feet were warm, but other than that, she was freezing. She had been standing with Dylan for hours on the side of the road, nibbling on crackers that Dylan had found a few hours ago. It was six in the morning, and Macey was starting to feel cold, hungry, and sleepy at the same time.

'Are you cold?' he questioned, carefully. 'Would you like my jacket?' he didn't wait for a reply—he was already shrugging out of it.

'N-n-no,' Macey chattered, her jaw clenched tight. 'You keep it. You might feel cold. I'm fine.'

'Macey. Be realistic. I'm a BC—I don't feel cold as easily as you do. Now here,' he sighed, wrapping the thin leather jacket around her. It didn't make much of a difference, but it felt nice, so Macey didn't argue.

'Do you mind if we go somewhere now?' Macey didn't understand what the point was of sitting just a mile from the mansion that she had just escaped from.

'Sure. Where do you want to go?'

'Well…is it possible to stay at a hotel or something until nine or ten, and then set out to find my family?' she half mumbled, half whispered the last part, afraid Dylan would say no. To her shock and pleasure, he agreed.

'I know a great place we can stay,' he shouted, so the zooming vehicles nearby didn't drown him out. Even at six a.m., the streets were crowded. The streetlights twinkled brightly, painting images on the smooth, almost metallic road made for gliding vehicles. BCs roamed around, filling up the streets, laughing and chattering. Nobody seemed to notice the human, which was odd but pleasant at the same time. 'Let's go!' continued Dylan, as a pack of motor bikers whooshed by, submerging his voice in the roaring sound.

He got up, his white shirt glimmering in the moonlight. His jeans were baggy and loose, and hid half of his faded black sneakers. Macey got her first chance to study his face. She'd already caught the brown eyes and light auburn hair, but she studied the details this time. Dylan's face stood smooth and rough at the same time—like sour candy. His cheekbones were clear, and his skin was a beautiful shade of tan.

Macey got up on her feet and followed awkwardly behind Dylan, who moved with swift movements. While walking, Macey was careful to observe that all the cars, if she could call them that, didn't seem to have steering wheels—they were just like the strange machine that brought her to this place.

Macey and Dylan only had to cross a few roads before they came across a glistening, towering hotel. Sparkling lights, posh doormen, elaborate rooms. At the entrance stood a huge, shimmering sign that read the words Hotel Hillary. Underneath, seen in tiny font, it read 'Luxury Begins Here'.

'Ooh. Fancy,' Macey gushed. They walked inside to find something totally unexpected. It was beyond luxury. It was beyond words. BCs stood at the bar, laughing and gossiping. Out on the dance floor—yes dance floor—they were dancing gracefully. The sound setup was booming strange tunes, some with frequencies that only BCs could appreciate. There was also an arcade, which was releasing beeping and shooting sounds. BCs were swimming in the heated pool, and were giggling all the time.

And the rooms. They were the best part. Two comfortable, cozy looking beds took little room in the enormous suite. There was a drinks machine, two electronic holographic zones, a shower, a bathtub, three sinks, a few vanity mirrors, and a fold out bed/sofa.

'Oh gosh!' she exclaimed. 'Dylan, I wanted to stay for a few hours, not a few years! It'll be a curse to leave this place.'

'That decision is up to you,' he smiled, revealing his perfect teeth. They clashed so well with his bronze skin.

Macey thought about it. As much as she wanted to stay in the sumptuous Hotel Hillary, she wanted to see her family more. She couldn't believe she'd gone without Leslie and Tim for what seemed like forever, and yet she was only ripped on the inside. 'Can we please go into bed now? I want to get as much sleep as possible before our big breakthrough,' she yawned, already crawling into the bed closest to the door.

'I already slept the two hours I needed to. You go ahead,' Dylan lied. 'I'll go down to the dance floor or something. Good night.' His hand was already on the knob, and he was almost out the door.

'Good night Dylan. I'll be awake by nine or ten,' Macey sighed, as she lost the battle with her heavy lids. Soon enough, she fell into a long, dreamless sleep.

When Macey woke up, she was completely stiff, which probably meant she hadn't moved at all during her peaceful sleep. She also woke up a little later then she planned, because the sun was almost directly overhead—almost noon. 'Dylan?' she muttered under her breath.

'Right here,' he commented. He appeared as if he never left at all. He was even wearing the same clothes. 'So what did you decide? Stay or leave?'

'Leave,' Macey confirmed. 'I want to locate Tim and Leslie. You know—my dad and my sister.'

'You have a sister?'

'Well, she's my best friend. And she's very, very pretty,' Macey sighed, her comment out of place. An image of Leslie was forming in her head. Her blonde locks radiating in the sunlight, her blue eyes illuminating happiness—she was such a fun person to be around. Macey couldn't wait to see her again.

Dylan snorted. 'Okay let's make you happy, princess,' he proclaimed sarcastically while getting up. 'We're going to Forbidden Earth.'

'You can't do that!' Macey screamed, scrambling to her feet. Dylan looked confused for a moment. When his words came out, they came out slowly, like he was trying to understand.

'What are you talking about? You just said you wanted to go,' he asked stupidly.

'The virus,' Macey said, placing her hands on her hips. She rolled her eyes as if it was obvious, and it was almost silly for Dylan not to get it. To Macey's shock, Dylan broke out laughing.

'Not you too! That whole idea is driving me nuts! Please tell me you don't believe in that bogus rumour, Macey,' he tried to stifle his laughter.

'Well I do. And you could fall sick,' she said, defensively.

'Don't worry,' he chuckled, his eyes still mocking her. Macey looked hurt for a second, but got over it quickly.

'All right then, let's go get ready,' said Macey. She grabbed the one shirt that she managed to stuff into Dylan's bag before they escaped and tossed it over her shoulder carelessly. Although she appeared smug, she had a bad feeling brewing somewhere deep inside her.

'How in the world will we get to Forbidden Earth?' Macey knew that it was an abandoned region. Dylan just smiled. The look in his mischievous eyes said *Leave it all to me.*

'No Dylan. I won't let you risk your life for me.'

'Who said I was risking my life?' asked Dylan, as one of his perfect eyebrows arched upwards. 'I'll be right back.' Before Macey got a chance to answer, Dylan was ripping down the glowing streets of Northern Earth.

Macey was really starting to get agitated at the way Dylan was behaving so far. She did whatever he said. The thoughts were clogging up her brain, and she felt like she was so thirsty, she would pass out right outside Hotel Hillary.

Macey was upset for a reason she couldn't quite grab. She knew she should be grateful for all Dylan and Emma had done for her, but wouldn't it be better if they never had to make the effort in the first place? They wouldn't have to rescue her if she didn't need rescuing, right? Macey's brain started to throb. Her stiffened arms reached upwards and came down slowly in an awkward form of a stretch.

Macey forcefully pulled her limp legs over the curb of the street, baking in the sudden heat. How could the weather change so fast? But in a way, the warmth felt good. The first ray of sunshine she'd experienced since she was captured. You didn't get that kind of luxury around the spaceship.

Her hands pulled across her chest, forming a giant X over her shirt. The jeans she was wearing were the same ones she was wearing the night of the escape. Her worn sneakers didn't seem like they could survive much longer without bursting at the size of Macey's grown feet. Her shirt was a red and green plaid design, something a child would wear on Christmas. The button-up top was firm and linty after being worn and washed so much. Her sleeves reached her elbow, scorching Macey in the unexpected rays.

Macey stared out at the street before her and realized something else. The BCs weren't driving cars, they were controlling devices that vanished and appeared in a blink of an eye. They were arriving in and out of nowhere.

Suddenly, Dylan was right in front of her eyes, inside one of the strange, moving devices. This one was probably the shiniest, newest one Macey had seen so far. It had a red colour that reflected the sun and blinded everybody around it. There were two, solid stripes painted down the side—one black and one white. It looked like something a celebrity would ride.

'Wow Dylan,' she nodded her head with approval. 'That was faster than I expected.' Her eyes reflected sarcasm at every level.

'Don't act shocked,' he grinned smugly, his hands in his pockets. 'You know what I'm capable of.' Macey just gawked at him. How could he be so proud of himself?

'I'm tired of arguing with you. You barely do anything. Now step on it!' Macey scoffed. She opened the door, careful not to ruin the stainless steel that the handle was made of. She sat down slowly, sitting as far away from Dylan as possible. If it was the last thing she did, she wouldn't let Dylan control her like this. Dylan looked bemused and laughed at Macey's attitude.

'Step on what?' he suddenly murmured, looking around. His eyebrows scrunched together, forming wrinkles in his smooth forehead. His voice caught Macey in a trance again, and she was amazed at how easily influenced she was.

Macey looked over at Dylan, to find the same white shirt,

brighter and cleaner than ever. Macey wondered how this could be—she was certain there was no dry cleaning service in the hotel or anywhere nearby. His black leather jacket was fit snugly over his muscular arms, and his baggy pants were still looking loose and comfortable. Big, brown eyes stared back at her, pleading like a small puppy's.

'The—the pedal,' Macey said, still temporarily dazed. Her finger was pointing lamely at Dylan's foot. Dylan chuckled, his hand over his mouth. Macey's hands flew to her hips. 'Do you know how to drive?' she shot. 'Do you know whose car you're driving?'

'About the first question...' Dylan said skeptically. 'I don't really know how to drive.' Dylan eyed Macey slowly, arms ready to catch her if she passed out. What should he expect? A temper tantrum? Just a few words? Complete silence?

All of his questions were answered as a look of concern crossed Macey's face. In a flash, she was fuming. You could see the shaking running up and down her spine, eager to get out with her words.

'You don't know how to drive?' she gasped, her fists tight to her chest, fighting for control. 'You steal somebody's... machine..., you pull me through trouble, you give me a sliver of hope, and then you tell me that you don't know how to drive.' Dylan was utterly unbelievable. How could he do this?

'Relax Macey. I'm not supposed to know how to drive.' Macey's gasps were starting to grow unnaturally even.

'Not supposed to know how to drive, you say?' her head cocked farther and farther with each syllable. 'Then, I suppose, I'll be much safer in another vehicle with a driver I can trust.'

She was already holding the door open, one leg hanging off the seat. Suddenly it was Dylan's turn to grow annoyed.

'Oh, Macey don't be a drama queen,' he whined sourly, his shoulders shrugging. 'This is a teleporter. My mom's.'

Macey sucked in a breath and tucked in her stomach. Her arms loosened at her side, and she looked up in the direction of heaven. She appeared to be reciting a prayer. 'Oh, Dylan, I hope this is safe,' she sighed, pulling the door shut again.

Dylan revealed his commonly used conceited smile. 'Well, go ahead and ask me.'

Macey made a face. What did Dylan want now? She hated being asked to guess something, when somebody right next to her could tell her what she was trying to assume. 'Ask you what?' Macey pried. Her words were well annunciated, a result of the cautiousness apparent in her eyes.

'Ask me how the teleporter works,' Dylan stated the obvious, in a tone that offended Macey with ease.

Macey scrunched her nose in disgust. She purposefully covered her face in a sheet of soft hair, cowering away from what she wanted to fight so badly.

'I don't want to know,' Macey mumbled through her protective shield of dark strands. Dylan merely shrugged his shoulders lightly, and untangled his hands from the threads of his jean pockets. He wiggled his fingers around a bit before taking one thick finger and jutting numbers into the small pad in between them. Curiosity took over Macey's anger.

'What's that? What are you doing?' Macey gave up. Dylan laughed at Macey's pathetic attempt to stay mad.

'I told you it's a teleporter. It teleports us. What else?'

Macey had enough practice by now. She ignored the comment without showing any emotion. Thoughts of Dylan were still trying to sink into her brain, but Macey kept them afloat.

'Not that, brainiac. What are you shoving your dirty fingers into?' Dylan continued to smile and laugh while Macey attempted to rat him out. 'I want to know whose teleporter I'm sitting in this very second,' Macey hissed through gritted teeth. 'If you don't tell me right now, I'm leaving. Don't expect me to come out of the shadows for you.'

'I already told you that too,' Dylan said surely, with a nod of his head. 'It's my mom's. April's. That's why it's so great,' he boasted.

'Then I don't get why she adopted you,' Macey tried. Unfortunately, this rubbed on Dylan in a completely wrong way. He seemed to think about what he had just heard as he let it sink in.

'I guess you're right,' he pouted, his brown eyes pleading again. 'I'm a thief. I'm a lazy thief. I'm a lazy thief who's never there when she needs me.'

Macey stared in shock as she tried to understand what he meant. *Thief?* As far as Macey was concerned, Dylan had stolen nothing that she knew of. What could Dylan possibly have stolen?

'Dylan, you know that's not what I meant,' she said frantically, an apology growing in her eyes. Her arms were out in a hug that nobody accepted. Dylan looked hurt. He lowered his chin to his muscular chest and began to laugh. Macey was quite confused.

'Hah!' he gasped. He belted out laughs until he was out of air and his mocking sounds were nothing but silence coming out of his open mouth. He slapped his knee, his face turning red with laughter 'Gotcha.'

Macey groaned and wished—and not for the first time—that Dylan would stop joking around and get serious. She could swear that they had just been sitting in the teleporter for fifteen minutes. 'Seems like you keep forgettin,' Dylan couldn't continue, his laughter broke in too soon. He tried again and again until he finally choked out the words: 'Seems like you keep forgetting I'm a BC. I don't have many feelings. I won't be that offended at whatever you say to me, no matter how mean.'

This news shot through Macey, bouncing around her rubbery stomach. She recalled all the times she had tried to hurt Dylan, and how many times it didn't work. 'Okay, great, fantastic show. Now let's go.' Macey replied impatiently, arms loyally at her side again.

'All right,' he breathed. Dylan was still pretty hysterical while typing in the words 'Forbidden Earth' into the teleporter pad. The lit up pad's monotone voice replied roughly.

'Are–you–sure–you–would–like–to–visit–Forbidden–Earth?' it asked.

Macey sighed with relief. For a second, she was afraid Forbidden Earth was a place you couln't teleport to either. Dylan let out another small scoff, trying to hold his laughs in. He tapped on the red icon that said *Yes,* rather than the green icon reading *No.* Though it was allowed, it was clear that it was frowned upon to visit Forbidden Earth.

Macey was starting to burn again, her plaid shirt feeling tighter and more thick than normal. She consumed a large sum of air and used effort to roll her tired eyes. With her head tossed back over the seat, her hair fell in neat strands behind her. The bright sun made beautiful patterns in them.

Dylan began to calm down at the sight, and he stayed for a minute to watch Macey's lashes flutter back and forth, back and forth. 'Uh–Macey?' he stammered, upset to interrupt.

Soaking up all that she could in the warm sun, Macey didn't even bother to open her eyes as she replied. 'Yes?' She smiled at the stutter in Dylan's tone.

'Well, I'm going to teleport us now. Close your eyes.' He sighed as he realized how idiotic he sounded. Macey's eyes had been closed for a minute. If Macey had caught the lameness in Dylan's voice, she didn't seem to show it. Her shoulders fell into a relaxed position, and she pushed her seat to starting position again.

She lightly flickered her lids to put on a seat belt, and closed them tightly again. 'Forbidden Earth, watch out. Here we come!' The last thing Macey felt was the wind stomping against her soft cheek before she opened her eyes.

Macey let in a huge gulp of air as she discovered that they were at the same spot she had landed on a while ago in her spaceship. To the right, the gorgeous waterfall was starting to lose it's rush because of the heat building up in the summer air. However, no matter how much water was missing, it was no less beautiful than it was last time. The air around Macey was so fresh that it was overwhelming; Macey couldn't stop breathing it in. But best of all, the pond into which the falls flowed was an amazing swirl of white and blue. It's pale colour made the growth and ferns around it pop out even more. For a second—just for a second—Macey stopped breathing in the fresh air to admire the artistry that bloomed in front of her very eyes.

'Dylan. You're absolutely amazing,' she whispered, her arms leaning out so far out of the vehicle she was about to topple out. How could such an amazing place be home to all the viruses the BCs were afraid of?

'I have a feeling none of this was my doing,' he choked.

Macey's perfect brows scrunched together to form two arches on her tan forehead. Distress dragged across her face, but vanished as she realized that she was probably falling for another one of Dylan's tricks. She bothered to ask anyway. What was the worst that could happen?

'What's wrong?' she asked, smoother and more sternly than expected. She almost convinced herself that she cared. But, instead of cracking a joke, all Dylan did was clear his throat before replying with a simple 'Nothing.'

Macey didn't look convinced, but she erased the look off her face anyway.

'What's next captain?' Dylan shouted, two fingers to his head in some form of a salute. 'Where can we find your family?'

Macey stopped short, breathing caught mid-throat. Realisation struck her like a tornado. This was the same place she had landed with her beloved Leslie and Tim. 'Dylan?' she asked slowly, her voice was about to crack. Dylan dropped his hand gently, trying hard not to trigger anything to make Macey's tears fall yet again. 'Is this the Lima Lake Waterfall? And Lima Lake?' Dylan could hear the worry inside Macey's voice.

Macey was recalling the map Leslie and Tim had used to find Earth while on the spaceship, as well as the map she found in the Presidential Palace. 'Dylan, my family is supposed to be here. Why aren't they here, Dylan? Why aren't they here?' Panic was growing insanely fast as she increased her speaking volume. She was gasping now, her face turning blotchy. Dylan stepped out of the vehicle quickly, and went to open the passenger door to help Macey out.

Dylan tried to reply calmly, but you could hear the edge of fear in his voice. 'I'm sure they must be here somewhere. We just have to look.' Macey clung to Dylan's shirt for support, as if not to pass out from fear, worry, and panic all at once. Her devastated face matched perfectly with her hunched back and limp walk.

Her lids dropped lightly, and Macey waited for further explanations from Dylan. Breathing was getting harder, and she heard Dylan's teeth grind in frustration right before he gulped.

Macey's eyes flew open at an amazing speed. 'What happened?' she whispered, still in an aloof mode. She moved her gaze around a bit and settled it softly on Dylan's shuffling foot. It was causing alterations in the perfect circle that was engraved into the muddy grass. The circle stretched for yards around, and Macey couldn't see the end of it. Inside it, you could see intricate patterns, as well as marks outside the circle that looked like....

Macey stopped short, everything inside her freezing. It was a spaceship's print. A giant spaceship's print. That could only mean one thing. One very upsetting thing that Macey would rather not think about. All that it meant was that Leslie Stevens and Tim Johnson were gone.

Dylan looked up and realized Macey knew everything. His face showed worry, and his body was tense. 'Macey...'

'Don't,' she started, the corners of her lips turning down. She started to turn before she burst into tears. 'Just don't!' she cried, running off into the blazing sun. Her hands were cupped over her eyes, and she was following the same path she'd struggled on when she was first captured.

∾

10

Decisions

Dylan had been searching for Macey for a while now, but to no avail. 'Macey!' he wailed one last time. 'Sorry!' he pleaded, though he knew both of them were well aware it wasn't Dylan's fault at all. His arms were cupped around his mouth and his eyes reflected failure on every level. 'Macey,' he finally mumbled, his hands falling pathetically to his sides.

Dylan's auburn hair shook around him as he plopped himself onto a nearby tree stump. He looked up into the wide branches above him. The whispering limbs were old, an indication of knowledge and wisdom. 'What've I done? I never should've come here in the first place,' he scolded himself. A shiver raced up his spine and Dylan sat for a moment, trying to escape the unfortunate world.

'Hi,' a light voice sniffed. Dylan, looking relieved, glanced up to see Macey's blotchy face staring down upon him. He smiled.

'Hey, sorry about your family,' he murmured, careful not

to trigger Macey's tears again. To Dylan's surprise, all Macey managed was a meagre smile.

'What's done is done. I can't change it, can I?' she sounded like she was still convincing herself.

'No, I guess not, but...,' Dylan started.

Macey cut him off. 'Okay then.' She sounded a lot more confident this time. The two sat quietly for a moment, both opening their mouths, and shutting them before a sound was released.

The silence was ripped apart when Dylan suddenly asked for a walk on the beach.

'I don't know,' Macey questioned. 'I've never been to a beach before...and...and you could fall sick.' Before Macey could protest any longer, Dylan had her on off the ground and into his strong arms without batting an eye.

'Do you still want to sit here alone?' Dylan smiled. Macey gawked with wide eyes, and shook her head soundlessly.

'Good,' Dylan said softly. 'Let's go, Macey.'

Macey walked quietly, but she was still unstable. 'Dylan, I've never seen a beach. Are they pretty?'

'That's for me to know, and for you to find out,' Dylan shouted. His voice still sounded quiet trying to top the rush of the cascading water. They were back at the spot where they started, right next to the teleporter.

Macey was almost certain they were lost, but Dylan seemed to know what he was doing. There was no paved road to follow in Forbidden Earth, which was no shock. Macey had asked quite a few times if Dylan really knew what he was doing or where they were going. And if he did, how did he?

'Macey Johnson, stop it right now!' Dylan always replied in a harsh tone.

But the ranting and arguing was worth it once Macey caught sight of the ocean's blue water. Her heart beat a mile a minute.

The blue colour rippled in the dim light; it was almost twilight. The beautiful water stretched as far as the eye could see, foaming under the setting sun. The ocean was rich with different colours—anything from blue to green to grey.

White water reached out from the sea, trying to grab Macey. After giving up, the tides would fall back and disguise in the ocean's depths. The sound of crying seagulls was in the air, loud and shrill, and the smell of salty water filled the atmosphere. With unmistakable beauty, the horizon met the setting Sun's glow at such a perfect angle. Macey could see how spherical and flawless the Earth really was.

The sand under Macey's feet, on the other hand, was warm and soft. The substance felt new and inviting. At first, Macey was frightened to enter the water, wondering if she would fall into the wet stretch in front of her, gone forever. But, as she edged herself towards the slippery, wet sand, the icy water felt refreshing.

For the third time that day, Macey didn't dare to breathe. 'Oh, God. How does this happen, Dylan? Where does all this water come from?' By the time she ripped her eyes from the nature before her, Dylan had his hands over his lips.

'Shush. Don't speak. Enjoy this moment while you have it,' he said, smiling crookedly. Without replying, Macey turned her head back to marvel at the ocean some more.

There was a warm breeze in the air; not too hot, not too cold. Though the ocean was as cold as ice, the Sun was still out there. A shiver of warmth spread out all over Macey's body. For the first time in a month, she was at complete ease. She savored the moment, though it didn't last long.

'Come on,' Dylan whispered, barely audible against the roaring waves.

'Where are we going?' Macey said.

Dylan didn't respond. He grabbed Macey by the hand and pulled her towards the water. But he didn't do what Macey thought he would. They walked up a soggy wooden staircase, sand filling every inch of their shoes. As they neared the end of the large, wooden platform—that appeared long abandoned— they approached a rusty iron fence.

Dylan cleared his throat before hopping the barrier in one swift movement.

'Whoa,' Macey said unevenly as she lurched over the fence herself. 'That was...interesting,' she commented, smoothing her shirt. Dylan turned one end of his lip up. But even after running one obstacle, Dylan was persistent on breaking more rules.

They dawdled together all around the rocky ledge, Macey acting cautious, as not to take a single wrong step. Dylan, however, walked with a large stride, barely looking under his feet. 'Please tell me this is over,' Macey pleaded.

Dylan reached into his pocket and took out two cameras. He kept one for himself, and tossed the other one to Macey. 'Here, use April's. You do know how to use a camera, don't you?' he teased.

April's camera was a dark purple colour, glistening in the bright light. It was small, covering half of Macey's petite hand.

'Yes,' Macey lied, trying not to seem stupid. She'd never held something with so many buttons before. The only more complicated thing she'd seen in her life was Tim's control room. The thought of Tim almost brought her to tears, but she kept those feelings away, for Dylan's sake.

'I'm sure you just press a few buttons, like this one...' Macey continued, pressing the smallest button she could see.

Dylan laughed. 'That's the slideshow button. You really don't know how to work this thing, do you?' he asked. Macey shook her head in dismay. She handed the camera back to Dylan. 'Why don't you just start it up for me, I can figure it out from there,' she said. Macey kept her head down, staring at Dylan through her thick, dark lashes.

After the camera was in his hands, Dylan's hands flew like bullets over the camera's buttons. He handed it back, a smile painted across his face. 'Whoa,' Macey breathed. 'This is incredible.' She held the camera to her eye, and everything she saw was mirrored exactly through the lens.

But she still wasn't satisfied. Looking through the camera lens, she still couldn't capture all the beauty at once. She still had to try her best.

Curious, Macey fiddled with another button. The screen instantly changed from the image of the blue water to a picture of a beautiful woman in a topaz dress. 'Dylan, who is this?' she asked, leaning over to hand the camera to him. Was it possible he had a love life? But the woman was so much older than he was.

Dylan's camera wasn't quite as beautiful from the outside; it was plain black. It was also quite chunky, and its neck-strap hung loosely around his neck.

Somehow, his pictures looked a lot more real to Macey. They had the same spark that she couldn't seem to capture. Ignoring the fact for now, she focused on Dylan's answer.

'Oh,' he said. 'She's my mom, April. Pretty, isn't she?' Macey gasped. She couldn't believe it. *That's where Dylan gets his looks from*, she thought with a smile. Suddenly, she put her fingers to her lips.

'I didn't say that out loud, did I?' she asked, slightly embarrassed.

'You did,' Dylan murmured with a smile. 'But you're wrong. I'm adopted.' His voice ended in a whisper, his head turning to take a few more pictures.

'Oh, Dylan I'm so sorry,' she gasped. She would never know what he felt like, but she was sure it must feel horrible not to know your real parents. Her fingers opened from her tight fist for a second, but returned to their position shortly afterwards. This time, she thought of Leslie. She had always been so private about her life away from Macey; it was like she didn't have one at all. *Why do I keep messing up?* Macey scolded herself.

Think about the bright side. 'Dylan, you're a really good photographer. How long have you been taking pictures?' To Macey's relief, her compliment made Dylan smile.

'Thanks. I taught myself nine years ago. I started when I was ten,' he beamed.

Macey realized pleasurably that Dylan was only one year

older than her. 'That's neat,' she said. 'Well, I'm not very good at this,' she laughed, referring to April's camera.

After returning April's camera back to Dylan, Macey walked as close to the edge of the cliff as possible, careful not to step on any loose stones. She sat down; the ledge was actually quite comfortable.

'Ah,' she sighed, her shoulders relaxing. Her legs dangled freely over the cliff's edge, hiding the monstrous beast beneath her. Her toes were tense, though; careful to keep a firm grip on the sneakers she was wearing. She couldn't afford to lose those.

The waves almost appeared to be crawling up the rocks, trying to grasp Macey's ankles. This fact barely bothered Macey now; she was used to it. In fact, it felt kind of relieving… almost powerful. Watching the waves struggle against the rough surface was quite entertaining, once she thought about it.

Her heavy eyes shut and as she lost herself in another world, Macey also seemed to lose track of time. Quickly and quietly, she fell into a calm, dreamless sleep.

11

─∞○∞─

Settling Down

When Macey fluttered back to life again, she realized she had been out for an hour; she wasn't too sore. It appeared to be night. She wondered where she was at first, and why she was wrapped inside a light blue blanket instead of her purple one at home.

The second the salty smell attacked her nose, she was surprised she had ever forgotten where she was. How could she not recall something so grand, and so beautiful?

She rolled over so she was lying down on her stomach. As Macey craned her neck upwards to gaze at the tinkling stars, she spotted Dylan leaning over the edge. She looked down at her own base, fearing she was inches away from falling over the ocean. To her horror's relief, she realized that yet again, Dylan had saved her.

Macey was tempted to shout out to Dylan, but was mesmerized for moments by the full moon that lit up the bright night sky. The stars glistened in myriad numbers, reflecting a dim but beautiful light across the blue water. The wispy palm trees could be heard in the slight breeze, but could not be seen. Like a mysterious force that was always surrounding them.

Macey turned her head down, feeling nauseous. After a couple of moments, when Macey looked up again, she found Dylan staring straight into her eyes. Curiosity rang through them. Quickly, Dylan cleared his throat and got up. 'Sorry,' he murmured. 'Just comparing your eyes to the stars.' He shot his hand through his hair. *A nervous habit,* noticed Macey with a smile.

She cleared her throat as well, debating whether or not to bring up the topic of her family again. Macey felt like she was just being a pain in the butt for Dylan, after all that he was doing for her. She couldn't dare face those emerald eyes again, could she? Instead, Macey decided on a mellower topic.

'When are you planning to sleep?' she yawned, her arms reaching towards the stars. Macey was sitting up, her hair in a tangled mess. Dylan didn't bother to reply.

'Dylan?' Macey asked, her voice bothered. Dylan peered up for just enough time for Macey to catch a glance at his face. He was deep in thought; it was obvious. He, too, appeared distraught. It was as if he was lost in the stars, his own little world where nothing mattered. Suddenly, Dylan shook his head, erasing all his previous thoughts from his head.

'What's wrong?' Macey asked, her eyes growing wide. Dylan hesitated before telling her what was on his mind.

'Macey, I think we both know your family won't be showing up any time soon,' he stammered. Macey knew what Dylan was saying was true, but it sounded so strange coming out of somebody else's mouth.

It took a while for Macey to respond again. The utter shock of the truth had stunned her once again, like a lightning bolt that was always twisting its haunting limbs through her soul. Her balance was lost along with this lightning bolt, as she stumbled backwards, nearly tumbling over the handrails.

Macey turned around barely fast enough to catch herself. *I'm officially, most definitely, the unluckiest human to ever live,* she thought.

'Yeah Dylan,' she said with a pang, 'I guess you're right...' she ended the sentence with a shake of her head. Her hair fell over her shoulders, suddenly even more tangled because of the strong wind. She lay there, panting. It suddenly seemed to grow extremely cold—almost freezing.

'In that case, we should settle nicely. A beach house with a view of the sunset each evening, maybe?' Dylan tried. Personally, Dylan would much rather live in the middle of the forest, where nobody could spot them, and they could be protected from the strict laws of their world. But anything would be better if it could make Macey happy.

Macey, on the other hand, didn't want to settle down at all. It just had such a negative ring to it, emphasising that there was no hope whatsoever of her father returning. But she couldn't be so picky when Dylan had already done so much for her, could she? *No,* she decided. *I can't do that to him. He only means well.*

'Alright. Sounds good to me,' she sighed, turning so she was facing Dylan again. Almost like a light bulb, Dylan's face lit up immediately at her acceptance.

'Great!' he explained, taken aback. 'I mean...great,' he added in a hushed whisper, slightly embarrassed. Macey laughed, surprising both of them. But her face darkened, almost as quickly as it had enlightened. Her tinkling laughter hung in the air, making the moment more awkward than it already was.

Dylan was the first to break the silence. 'Well, I guess we should go down for the night,' he cleared his throat.

Macey grunted. 'I just slept. You go ahead. I'll join you later. Just give me a moment by myself,' she sighed, her warm breaths apparent against the chilly air. She wrapped her arms around her own shoulders, rubbing them against her soft shirt. Macey leaned forward, until her elbows were resting on the stone railing. The wind whipped through her hair. The whole effect was so dramatic, it was crazy.

It took Dylan a chance to break the moment. 'I'll, um, get the temporary shelter ready, um, for the night,' he scurried away, face flushing.

'Who's a good little girl? Who's a goochigoochi goo?' Dylan touched the soft fist. Macey and Dylan had probably been living together for a while now. During this period, Macey had given birth to twins, a boy and a girl, fathered by Dylan. They named the girl Kimberly, and the boy Logan. The two had taken on their father's last name: Brown.

Macey was sleeping at the time; she seemed a lot more tired since the twins were born. Now, Dylan realized that the reward of a painful couple of months was worth it.

Kimberly had beautiful, crystal blue eyes that went so well with her dark brown hair. It was a rare combination, and gorgeous when it was found. Logan, on the other hand, had pale hair and dark eyes. A more common look. Still, taking care of the children was a new experience for both Dylan and Macey. What made it more interesting was the fact that they were both combinations of both a human and a BC. But as far as the two could tell, Kimberly had the smarts and the immunity, while Logan had neither. But one thing they both had in common was the most valuable of all: emotion. Emotion was something Dylan was also learning to develop as he spent more time with Macey.

'What?' Macey replied drowsily, facing the wall of their small, temporary apartment. Dylan had built it near the sandy beach; he knew Macey enjoyed the feeling of having the ocean as a front yard. The whole 'house' was like something out of a house decorating magazine. The outside was like some sort of a hut, with a hay roof and thin walls. The inside had the basic necessities: a bathroom, two beds, and a small kitchen. As for furniture, it wasn't the best. After all, what did they have to make it out of?

'It's already three. You should wake up now, it's your turn with the kids,' Dylan whispered. With renewed energy, Macey opened her eyes and lifted her head off of her stiff pillow. Steadily, she made her way towards their home-made cribs and lifted Logan to her bosom. She was careful; she hadn't seen much practice parenting back on her spaceship.

'Da dadadumdum,' Logan giggled happily, waving his tiny

fists in the air as drool dribbled down his plump chin. He barely had any hair on his soft head, and his cheeks were so chubby they looked like full donuts. Macey couldn't help but smile. Logan was so stupid, but equally cute.

'Let's go out,' Dylan said. 'For a walk.'

'As long as you promise to bring the stroller,' Macey was referring to the small basket they used to carry the two miracles. Dylan laughed and pretended to throw Kimberly in the air before planting her in her spot in the tiny basket.

'Come on,' Dylan said, already halfway through the door.

Walking along the ocean shore was definitely not a new thing anymore, but for some reason, it felt different with the twins. Like there was some connection with the ocean's treasures and the children's acceptance. Or perhaps it was just the fact that spring was coming along, and flowers were blooming. Puffed blossoms sprouted near the tree growths, and bright bees buzzed around them at an amazing speed. Macey had seen pictures of these tiny black and yellow beauties.

Suddenly she heard a cry come from Dylan's direction. 'Oww!' he screamed, his hand on his forearm. 'Ow, ow, ow, owww,' he said again, this time hopping around.

'What's wrong?' Macey asked leisurely, cradling the basket in her arms. She was sure he had just stepped on a twig or something.

'A bee just stung me!' Dylan cried, leaping in pain. Macey had never felt a bee sting, but she knew they were mostly harmless. For humans, at least.

'So?' Macey teased. 'Is the sting too bad?' Macey shut up when Dylan revealed his arm. It was swollen to an immeasurable extent, and was as red as a tomato during harvest season. 'Whoa, Dylan this is not good...' Macey trailed off, while trying not to appear too worried at the sight of his sting's reaction.

'What do I do Macey? You're the human! You're immune to this stuff, aren't you?' Suddenly a thought occurred to Macey.

'Logan and Kimberly!' she screamed. 'Their immunity systems aren't well developed!' Macey was sobbing, Dylan was shouting, Logan was whimpering, and as a result of all the chaos, Kimberly was on the verge of tears. 'Where are we going to find a doctor now?'

Suddenly a hush fell over the four of them. Even the kids shushed up at the sound of Macey's voice. Macey thought she'd seen this scene many times before. She was certain Dylan would start fake crying, run off into the sunset dramatically, and then they'd have an even more emotional reunion. But that didn't happen this time. Instead, Dylan began to twitch uncontrollably.

'Can't...stop...myself...,' he said in a raspy whisper. Immediately after that, he got thrown into a mysterious coughing fit, letting out bursts of air until he couldn't breathe anymore.

'Dylan! This isn't supposed to be happening!'

'Well...maybe...you...aren't...the...brightest...species... either,' Dylan replied smart-alecky, referring to Macey's comments about immunity.

'I can't let you go through this,' Macey said, ignoring his sarcastic remark. 'I'm calling the Medical BCs. And there's nothing you can do to stop me.' Macey was hugging both

Logan and Kimberly in her arms now. 'Logan and Kimberly won't survive these bees either.'

Suddenly, Dylan's twitching stopped abruptly. 'No! Y-you can't d-do that!' This time, he stuttered with worry and guilt. 'I-I won't let you!'

'Fine. I'll only wait if you promise to stay indoors at all times, and to never go near the kids. Just in case it's contagious.'

Dylan felt like his heart had just cracked in half. 'B-but it's not contagious! I swear!'

'That's the deal. You either let me call the hospital right this moment, or you stay away from the kids until you feel better. If you feel better.'

Dylan sighed. It was a small price to pay for their safety. He was sure he could pull through at least a year, if it meant saving Macey, Logan, and Kimberly. 'Fine,' he agreed.

∾

12

Planning in Space

Leslie and Tim sat speechlessly as they hovered over two plates at a table for two in one of the spaceship cafes. Their hands fluttered nowhere near the untouched plates of stale bread and bowls of cold soup. The chattering people around them talked loudly, probably discussing Macey's capture and Tim's decision to take off without her.

Tim looked too big for the table he was seated at; his knees bent up too far when he sat down, and his arms fell too low off the sides of his chair. 'Leslie, I can't take it anymore!' he rumbled, causing the table to shake. Leslie kept her hand wrapped against her forehead, her elbow resting on the table. With her other hand, she rubbed her sleepy eyes.

'We have to go back and find Macey! This is horrible!' he continued to thunder. 'Being the captain, I did what I had to do to save all the lives I am responsible for. But these last few years have been a torture. I need to get my daugter back.' Leslie smiled gratefully.

'Tim, I knew you'd come around. Promise me that we'll land our spaceship back on Earth. I need my soul sister back,' she said.

All Tim responded with was a scratchy sound originating from his hungry throat. 'I vow not to eat anything until I have Macey safe in my arms again,' he challenged himself, knowing this was probably a promise he couldn't keep.

After a few moments, Tim stood to stretch his brawny legs and yawned. His arms stretched far above his head and came down slowly to relax his tense muscles. He sighed.

'Let's go up to my office. We can discuss a plan there,' Tim offered. Leslie agreed, ignoring the cries of her hungry stomach.

Leslie followed Tim up the stairs and tried to think of the whole situation from Macey's point of view. Wouldn't she miss her dad? But then Leslie realized: she didn't have to imagine. She was living through the exact same things. Leslie's parents had abandoned her long ago, and she wondered where they were that very second. Were they still alive? Were they on another spaceship? What did they look like? Where did they come from?

Leslie let the thought slip and shifted her attention to the loving dad in front of her. She knew Tim meant it when he said he wouldn't eat until he could find Macey. But she also knew that both of them were well aware that if that was the case, Tim might not eat again. He might value his life more than his promise, but it was more likely that if he couln't be with Macey, he wouldn't want to 'be' at all.

Once the two reached Tim's office, Leslie sat herself down

in the The Dare Chair yet again. Together, the two took a deep breath, both knowing this conversation was the conversation that would determine their future life with Macey.

The office was rather clean now. Well, it was really clean. All the books were organised in alphabetical order by author. The items inside Tim's desk were filed neatly by category. The pillows that lay near the reading bench were properly fluffed. The walls even reeked of a new coat of paint.

Leslie was quite impressed by Tim's change in behaviour. Her best guess was that, since Macey was gone, the guy had a lot of spare time. He probably attempted changing his surroundings to try to forget her, but he soon figured out that he couldn't.

Tim let out a relieving sigh as he sat himself down on the cushioned reading ledge. His legs stretched far out in front of him and his toes touched the wall opposite to the one his back rested against.

He closed his eyes as he let out another breath, slowly and quietly. His shoulders relaxed and his hands were placed against his empty stomach. Leslie could swear he was imagining Macey. Leslie followed his lead, but kept her eyes open to record the moment. She hadn't seen Tim any happier in the past few weeks.

A slow grin stretched across Tim's softened face. 'Oh, yes please, Macey,' he mumbled. His voice was so low and quiet, Leslie could barely hear it even in the silence of the abandoned hall. She was certain Tim was recreating their first tea party— Leslie and Macey had only been seven at the time.

Leslie traced the grooves of her hand in a fashion so

familiar, she wondered if somebody had done that to her before. 'Mom' was the first word that came to her mind. Her topaz eyes glistened in the dim light as she squeezed her hands together tightly. She let out an uneven breath as a single drop of water rolled down her cheek. Leslie's eyes flickered open to find that Tim was still lying down, his back to her now. Leslie didn't want to disturb him, so instead, she observed every detail around her.

She was wearing tight fitted jeans, showing off her slender figure. They matched well with her v-neck, even though she didn't have any interest in picking out her outfits since Macey's disappearance. Her flats were just the first things Leslie saw. They didn't go well at all with the rest of her clothes. The design showed bunches of yellow flowers with orange stems. The shoes were also decorated with two small orange bows at their tips. Leslie felt like a total clown.

Tim, however was dressed perfectly for the occasion. He had a cotton coloured button down sprawled across his brawny chest. The ends were not visible, for they were tucked into his ironed black pants. A blue and black tie hung from his neck as well.

'Tim?' Leslie breathed, still unevenly. 'Tim, let's go back and find Macey. I have a plan.' One of her knuckles rested in her other hands palm. They shifted oddly while Leslie kept her eyes down. 'What would happen if you joined the armed forces? For the BCs I mean.'

At last, Tim's lids revealed his brown eyes, happy at his thoughts, uncomfortable at their ending. He turned to face Leslie, but kept his head on the pillow. He looked torn.

Tim's eyebrows arched high above where they should be, breaking the moment. He guessed. 'I would be a traitor?'

Leslie chortled and tossed her head back so that all she could see was the freshly coated, cream coloured ceiling. Her arms moved from her chest down to the armrests of The Dare Chair and she twirled once. Her floral ballet flats served as a base when she pushed her legs off the floor. Leslie's purple v-neck had many wrinkles in them...her laundry was not her priority since Macey was gone. Unlike Tim, who was wise enough not to waste his time, Leslie spent her days mourning over something she knew couldn't be fixed.

Now's my chance to break through, she thought. Her plan seemed dangerous, but what was the worse that could happen? They would capture her and she would stay with Macey? That didn't sound so bad.

'If you joined the BC's army, then you would be trusted, right?' she questioned herself. Tim's face was still painted with doubts.

'And if they find out I'm human, I'm dead meat waiting to be cooked, aren't I?' he challenged.

'Wrong. You're prisinor. With Macey.' Leslie said. Suddenly she shook her head in disbelief. 'But that's Plan B. It's better to have Macey with us. Besides, what if she already escaped? Then we would be prisoners alone. What good does that do to us?'

Tim still didn't look convinced. 'What would I do with trust? How would I keep my identity a secret?'

'Just...don't hit the sack too much,' Leslie shrugged the problem off; it was minor in her mind. 'They'll never know! Please Tim,' she begged. She bent over to place her small hands in Tim's protection. She sat on her knees so her face was level with Tim's. 'For me.'

Tim sighed. 'Alright. But what am I supposed to do?' Leslie registered the good news and then broke out into a huge beam. Her smile stretched from the tip of one ear to the tip of the other.

'Yes!' she exclaimed. 'Yes, yes, yes!' Leslie stood and thrust her hands up into the air, twirling around in happiness. 'Thank you, oh, thank you so much.' Leslie returned to her squatting position, her head bowing in respect. Her voice lowered to a whisper as she completed her praise for the promise made.

Tim smiled politely, and his sad eyes perked up just a hair. *I'll do what it takes to get my daughter back,* he decided.

'Alright. If you join the armed forces, you'll be allowed inside the Presidential Palace...right?' Her face became suddenly serious and her shoulders tensed. She was shaking with anxiety.

Nodding in agreement, Tim wondered how far Leslie was willing to take this. Leslie wasn't even the main part of the plan. If the idea gave *her* shivers, what would it mean to Tim?

'Well, if you could kidnap the President, there would be chaos...right?' Leslie asked again, her attitude continuing throughout her speech.

'Oh, god, Leslie I guess that's right,' Tim tried. A puzzled look shone off his concerned face.

'Then...they wouldn't care who came in and out to check on Macey as long as they had an ID. Which—you would have as an armed professional. I mean, come on Tim. Who could refuse you?' Her small hands touched Tim's large bicep. She cocked her head. 'You're the man every army wants, no matter how much you sleep,' she ended her sentence with a smile, attempting to make a joke out of the serious matter.

As if to prove her point, Leslie stood, clapped her hands, and seated herself in Tim's desk chair. The leathery feel was cold and refreshing against Leslie's uncomfortable jeans, and the cushioned seat was unbelievably soft. She shut out the relieved feeling and braced herself on Tim's answer instead. His response was quick and simple.

'Yes,' he said. Leslie scrunched her eyebrows and returned to an attentive position again. She was ready to ask questions... there were a million different things Tim's response could've meant.

All Leslie's baffled expression received was a soft chuckle. Tim's smooth skin crinkled while his eyes mirrored fondness for Leslie. Leslie herself began to smile, because she couldn't help it. Tim's laugh was utterly contagious.

'Alright, alright, I think we're done goofing off for now,' Tim mused, thinking Leslie's plan was hopeless. Tim was sitting upright now, but his back was hunched over his legs, his elbows touching his knees. His arms were bent, but still extended out in front of him. As he looked up, Leslie was taken aback by the sparkle in his eyes. Tim hadn't laughed any more than half-heartedly for a while.

'Yeah,' Leslie trailed off. She kept her head angled at a position where she could bury her head into her hair at any time. She still wasn't sure what Tim meant. After a momentary silence, Leslie asked her awaited question. 'By yes, do you mean you'll continue with our plan?'

'Bet all your money I will,' he answered reassuringly. 'It doesn't seem like it'll work out too well, but hey, I have nothing to lose.' His calm tone put Leslie at ease almost instantly. Dazed, she stood, indicating the conversation was over.

Her head was spinning for a reason Leslie couldn't quite place. Either because she was still thoroughly exhausted, or she was this close to all her wishes coming true. Wanting to put everything off for tomorrow, she edged towards the large, wooden door.

As she walked out into the dim hallway, she waved two fingers as a farewell. Leslie didn't even bother to look back; she was too tired. As she passed the portraits of famous people in the hall, their fake smiles helped her realize one thing: at that moment she was utterly happy.

her; she handed the hammer to Tim and walked away from destruction for the day.

Now, they were hovering above Earth's atmosphere. They could land any second. The plan called for a landing about five miles away from where they landed last time. If they landed at the same spot, the whole scheme would be more obvious.

The suspense was killing as Leslie and Tim sat in the complicated control room. It was filled with hundreds of tiny buttons, switches, and bulbs. Although everything was organised in its own fashion, the complicated tinkers gave the whole room a messy sort of look. On top of that, it was a low-roofed, cheaply tiled place.

Everything was really ancient after providing humans with protection for hundreds of years. Tim claimed that when he was a young boy, he'd come down to the control room with his father. Together, they'd pretend Tim was a spaceship captain, just as he would be in the future. He would act like he knew what all the buttons were in charge of, flicking a switch every now and then. Once, he had accidently caused the shuttle to be in a total blackout for a week.

Thankfully, by now, Tim had it all figured out. The engines were ready to go, and at the flick of a switch, they would be fired at incredible speed.

'Let's do this thing!' Tim shouted, punching his fist the air.

'For Macey,' Leslie agreed, her eyes hovering over the control panel. She finally rested upon a switch that blended perfectly with its surroundings. Tim had identified that switch as their final move. After that, they would be heading towards Earth with supersonic momentum.

13

Preparations

'All set, Tim. Let's find a safe spot to land this time,' Leslie said, seated in the passenger seat of the control room. Everything was perfectly planned out. As soon as they landed, they would let the BCs see them. But instead of being captured, all the humans would help to fake an explosion. The illusion would be created by producing visual effects using projectors planted all around the spaceship.

'We'll make it as obvious as possible,' Tim nodded. There was only one problem. They couldn't land in the city. They had to be lucky enough to land during an aircraft flight, or in front of a security camera.

'But even if we don't get caught, the plan can still work. They'll never know we were even there if they don't catch us on tape or something,' Leslie pointed out. The idea seemed pretty foolproof to Leslie. What could go wrong? At the very worst, Tim could be caught as a human, but that seemed pretty unlikely.

Leslie and Tim spent hours working on the plan together; they would be devastated if it failed. Leslie swore they had covered every loophole in their major mission. At the end of each day spent working, they always chanted the same rhyme.

We miss you so dearly, we never forget,
The moments we've had, the day that we met,
The laughter, the memories, the love, and the joy,
Our love for you just cannot be destroyed.
For Macey.

Together, they performed the chant so many times; it was permanently carved into their heads. That's how long they spent working on their plan. The hardest part for them was destroying the spaceship. If the BCs came to investigate the scene and found the spaceship perfectly intact, what would they think?

It had taken a long time for Leslie and Tim to conduct that part. All the photographs in the hallways either had to be smashed to pieces on the floor or cracked to bits on the wall. The floor of each hallway was covered in ashes, to give the whole fiery explosion more of an effect. The cafe looked as if it had been turned upside down. Soup splattered all over the naked walls, coating it in a disgusting, drippy, yellow colour. Most of the old floorboards were easy to destroy; they were so flimsy. Leslie and Tim had fun ripping the floor to shreds and undoing every nail on each and every floorboard. The worst part, in Leslie's opinion, was hammering out the wall that she and Macey had painted together long ago. It was so hard for

As if to savour the moment, Leslie raised her hand dramatically. 'Let's have some fun while we're at it,' she joked.

Tim smiled and rolled his eyes. 'Alright, do your thing,' he sighed reluctantly. He gestured towards the button as he said it, and then looked away.

Leslie giggled. 'Tim, you're the best,' she laughed. All of a sudden she stopped, returning to her dramatic scene. Her hand quivered with anxiety, slowly inching closer to the small, white switch.

Her head bowed down, showing respect for the action about to take place as her fingers fell upon the switch. 'Three, two, one,' Leslie whispered. Outside of the spaceship, the two heard a sudden roar as it lurched forward, back towards their home planet.

Everybody else on the spaceship was in the evacuation room, which was built exactly for cases like so. There, people were provided with nothing but poles and seat belts to fasten onto for the fast trip back to Earth. It was dangerous for small children and newborns to be a part of the journey, but the risk had to be taken. The younger ones were seated mostly in their parents' laps, sharing a seat belt. Every seat was crammed, covering the beige seating completely. It was hardly beige anymore; it was so chipped.

Out of all the rooms, the evacuation room was probably the oldest on the space shuttle. There was no decoration effort put into it whatsoever. The entire room was a revolting cream colour, down to the very last seat buckle. There was no natural light at all; the room was entirely lit by wall lamps. They cast a yellow glow around everybody, causing their skin to look alien—like and unhealthy. It was every clean freak's nightmare.

The room was petite too, fitting about one hundred people at the most. If the entire capacity was used, the whole room would start to heat up to a temperature that would start to grow unbearable. To everybody's relief, the trip to Earth wasn't that long.

In fact, it only took a few minutes.

The spaceship flew at an utterly amazing speed; everything was a blur. Through the control room's windows, you couldn't see anything but pitch darkness until the shuttle whirred to a sudden stop. Leslie and Tim had guided the spaceship through Earth's atmosphere and were slowing down as they approached land. According to a map and reference books, they were landing in what used to be Central America a thousand years ago.

They still had a few miles to go, but from their elevation, the view was beautiful. Everything was a rich shade of green, and the hills looked so full of different hues. Although there was no water around like Tim and Leslie's previous destination, the view was still worth seeing; the moment worth capturing.

Leslie had her fingers crossed behind her back all the time. 'Come on, come on,' she prayed. The last thing she wanted was not to have to fake the explosion. The projectors were set to turn on the second their spaceship touched solid ground.

By now, Leslie and Tim were so close; they could almost smell the wet grass. It was bright outside, the most sunny they'd had in long time. 'Come on, Tim. We're almost there,' Leslie said, peering out of the windows.

Tim half smiled as he straightened out his plain white

t-shirt. Today he was dressed in military dress, enough to show off his stocky legs, but not enough to look too casual. He repeated the words under his breath, as if it were a magic spell. 'Almost there, almost there.'

Leslie hurried towards the public announcement system, stumbling across all the different buttons on the way. She was ready to inform all the passengers about their early arrival. Leslie hunched over the microphone, fingers light as if not to damage anything. Her voice remained serious and professional, but the happiness she had tried to hide was obvious.

'Attention everyone!' She paused for a moment, waiting to receive everybody's undivided attention. After she was certain she had waited long enough, Leslie proceeded with her announcement. 'Our main landing gears are about to hit ground. I repeat, our main landing gears are about to hit the ground!' she shouted the second time, falling into the chair behind her, microphone still in hand. 'Prepare for landing,' she whispered, taking a deep breath.

Leslie and Tim waited like birds in a nest as the announcement was carried throughout the echoing halls. All at once, chaos drove through the ship, sending it through like a wave. Footsteps could be heard stomping all over the purposely ruined floors.

Everybody found a comfortable position where they could still act crippled and weak. After Tim was out and safe in the world of BCs, all the humans would start a new life underground, occasionally coming to the back of the ship for extra food and water.

By the time the spaceship started inching towards the

ground, everybody was calm and quiet, ready for what was to happen next. Babies and young children were kept in the evacuation room; some risks had to be taken. Leslie stood by the window, watching for any sign of the BCs spotting them. Sure enough, she could see the gleam of a security camera lens through the lush trees. It was well hidden in the greenery, but the shine of it gave the secret away. The technology level was amazing, how cameras in the middle of nowhere could be reporting to the big city, ratting people like Leslie out.

Tim's breathing pattern was irregular; he was so nervous. Leslie couldn't blame him. Their stomachs were filled with butterflies; their minds overwhelmed with inexplicable hopes. Leslie leaned over until her head was resting on Tim's shoulder. 'Tim, be safe out there. For me.'

'Leslie, you've always been like a daughter to me. Stay that way for me when I come back,' Tim coughed. Although the statement was a sad one, it glimmered with hope. Tim had said he would come back, and he never lied. His honesty was finally being put to the test.

He touched Leslie's soft cheeks just in time to catch the perfect teardrop that was working its way to Leslie's chin. 'Tim I can't lose you too,' she sighed, pressing her hand on top of his. She planted a small kiss on his forehead before he left. 'Come back. Please.' Leslie whispered as Tim got up and started towards the door. He never looked back.

∾

14

_____∞∞∞_____

The Application

Leslie couldn't believe it. Tim was gone. He had vanished, almost as quickly as Macey did. It left Leslie wondering, giving her the same awed feeling that she had after watching 'Marc the Magician's Magnificent Magic Show' when she was twelve.

But since Leslie was suddenly on the spaceship, completely guardian free, she realized that Tim and Leslie were always thinking about the details. It never struck them that Leslie would become an only child, alone, underground, with a group of maniacs. Well, some maniacs. But Leslie knew more than to mourn. It was all for the best, wasn't it?

Although she didn't want to think about it, the situation kept popping up from the back of her head. Finally, Leslie gave up and decided to explore the ruined spaceship and check up on all of the passengers.

She was quite surprised to discover that there were really good actors/actresses on the ship. Leslie almost broke into tears after seeing some moaning, ash covered humans. She did run into a few people she knew too. Though, she was really just trying to keep her mind distracted from what it really wanted to think about. She strolled through the spaceship alone, praying the BCs wouldn't arrive at the scene. *They can't come so soon,* she reassured herself. But there was no knowing what had happened to technology on Earth while humans were gone.

As her mind wandered, so did her feet. Eventually, she ended up in Tim's office. She couldn't help it, of course.

The sentimental feelings were back twice as fast as it took to get rid of them. To add onto that, Tim had only been gone for a few minutes. *Come on, wimp.* She told herself. *You've been gone from Tim for days before. You're just fooling yourself.* It took a while, but Leslie convinced herself that the thoughts going on in her head were right. Cautiously, she took another step into the study.

She breathed a sigh of relief when she discovered nobody had dared pick Tim's office as their hiding spot. Leslie again sat down on the Dare Chair and twirled herself until she was completely tangled up in her thoughts. They clustered together in her head, moulding together and forming even more confusing thoughts. As she twirled for what seemed like the hundredth time, she suddenly stopped.

Underneath a loose floorboard, something was glimmering: something that she hadn't noticed before.

Step by step, Leslie inched the tip of her shoe towards the loose nail and ripped it open. It was a lot easier, since it had been loosened during the time of preparation. Underneath it lay a perfect brown book. The book was quite thick, almost 300 pages long. It was covered in smooth leather, bumpy but pleasant to touch. Curious, Leslie turned the book over, and touched the golden letters engraved into the cover. *Macey's Diary*, it read. Leslie's heart skipped a beat.

Macey kept a diary? How come Leslie never knew about it? How long had this been going on? Why was it underneath the floorboards? Everything was messed up. Leslie couldn't believe what she did next, or how long she would feel guilty about it, but she opened it up to the first page. Before she could read the first entry, she found something that didn't look at all like Macey's manuscript. Instead, there was a note written there in Tim's messy handwriting.

Leslie,

I see you have discovered Macey's diary. Be very careful. It means a lot to me, and to her. I'm sure it will mean a lot to you too. Hopefully, this book will spark some deep memories. Keep entertained. Be safe.

—Tim

A big, fat tear welled up in Leslie's eye, and—she knew she would regret this—she turned the page. There, Tim's handwriting was replaced by a neater manuscript.

How do I start this? Dear Diary? Just a simple hello? Let's just ignore the intro. Let me start my story.

Today wasn't the best day. I've felt better. The only ones who help me through this mess are Dad and Leslie. I can't imagine where I would be without them...

    I bet it's not too hard now, Leslie thought bitterly. She read on...

    ...They are my everything. The ones that help me get through this roller coaster called life. Today, I found out the truth about my mom. That no, she's not traveling constantly abroad other spaceships, searching for a better life for us. Or no, she's not staying in hiding for some secret reason that nobody bothered to tell me. But, she is gone. 'Watching over me in the clouds'. Dad says she never really left...that she was always in his heart. But how do I know that is not a lie either? I know I shouldn't be bothered; that he is supposedly going through pain as well. But what am I supposed to think? How am I supposed to react? Act like this whole thing is just a joke? It's not. It's just another day in my insanely real life. I'm only eleven. Do I deserve this? What did I do wrong? Well, welcome to my world.

—August 15, 3053

    By now, Leslie was totally intrigued. Macey had never shared her feelings in this form. But did that make her secretive? Weren't they best friends? It was all just so confusing. Puzzled, Leslie flipped onward.

    Today was my birthday. I didn't have that great of a time though, knowing that my mom could've been there with me. Dad did try to make it up to me, though. And the kitchen's head chef did make my favourite spaghetti and meatballs dish. But it didn't feel the same. Why couldn't Dad wait a day to tell me something he should've told me years ago? I waited this long. I could've waited another day.

—August 16, 3053

Leslie was torn between her feelings. Why wasn't there any mention of her? Macey's twelfth birthday had been such a blast. Did Macey feel differently? Leslie had worked so hard that year to make a three layer cake, complete with perfect icing. She even took the time to frost out the message 'Happy Birthday, Macey' in multicoloured dessert frosting. How long had Macey felt that way? But in a way, it was okay. It was Macey's diary. But did that give her the right to exaggerate? Confused beyond belief, Leslie turned another perfect page.

Why, oh WHY is my life filled with such unreliable people? I couldn't even trust Leslie today. I found out that she knew about my mom all along! And still, she didn't bother to tell me. Why is she keeping such big secrets from me? It wouldn't have hurt if she told me. It hurts more now. And she is my best friend...

—August 17, 3053

Leslie was startled. She had never felt that way. What was going on? The only reason she hadn't told Macey was because Tim had sworn it was only best for her.

Shattered, Leslie threw the diary onto the ash covered floor. 'Two can play this game, Macey!' she screamed, stomping out of the room. How could she think about saving such an ungrateful oaf now?

～

Meanwhile, Tim was making his way through the clumps of trees that surrounded him. The air around him was moist and humid, making beads of sweat appear on his forehead and the back of his neck. The second he chopped down a tree or tore apart a bush, the sun seemed to beat down harder and harder until it felt like the sun was Tim's only partner in life. As if the whole sky was a blazing fire wall. As he parted the dark green shrubs to the side, Tim couldn't help but try to imagine what lay on the other side.

His chocolate coloured eyes were fierce, mesmerizing the small squirrels and chipmunks for a moment before they scurried into the distance, never to be seen again. After what seemed like days, (though it had only been an hour), Tim walked through the last clearing.

It seemed like a dramatic moment, something Leslie would make a big deal out of. He raised his hand, prepared to slice through the leaves like a knife through warm butter. But as Tim cleared the path, he was faced with another fence. *Of course,* he thought. *Who wouldn't put a fence between a highway and a bunch of trees?* But before he climbed over, Tim added one last thought. *Hang in there, Macey. I'm coming.*

Finally, he pulled one leg over the tall, green barrier, halfway to freedom. As he pulled his head over and dropped the ground, Tim froze. In front of him stood two BCs; both with their backs to him. He looked down and cringed. It'd be hard to get by without making a sound; the ground was covered in fallen leaves and skinny twigs. *Please, stay quiet,* Tim prayed silently while inching slowly towards the bushes on the other side. What were the BCs doing on the side of the road anyway? Could they possibly have seen him through the video cameras and have arrived early? *Leslie,* a voice gasped in his head, urging him to turn back and run as if nothing had ever happened. But he knew better. And he prayed that Leslie did, too.

Slowly, like a burglar robbing in daylight, Tim stepped over a clump of still green leaves. The farther he looked, the older the leaves seemed to get. A few yards away from him, the middle of the leaves remained green. However, the edges crumpled inwards, brown and useless. He realized it was almost like staring into the future. What if his plan was useless and he ended up like the brown wilted leaves? What then?

Tim closed his eyes and gulped, looking at the BCs up and down. They were so still compared to the freeway, which was constantly moving; the BCs inside their vehicles probably never even glanced vaguely in their direction. Cautiously, Tim took another step. *Snap!* He heard a twig crack underneath him. He winced at the sound, knowing how it had given away his presence. At first the BCs were even stiller than before, their muscular stomachs barely moving as they breathed. But Tim wasn't fooled. He knew they were listening, like blind predators listening for his pray to make a single step. Slowly he saw them turn around, not fast enough to see his body cowering in the shadows just yet. Tim jogged a few steps backwards in an attempt to disappear with the shade, but the sound drowned his ears more than it needed to. *Snap! Crunch! Snap!* Tim cursed under his breath, but held on to the sliver of hope that the BCs would mistake his sounds for those of a squirrel or chipmunk.

It was too late. The BCs were out of their slow mode, rushing towards the bushes at incredible speed. Tim froze in his tracks and squatted, praying that he could disappear along with his confidence. As the muscled legs brought their way closer and closer to Tim's pounding heart, the pale haired teenager spoke. 'Al, who'd be here, in the middle of the freeway? I mean, of course we're here, but that doesn't give an excuse for somebody else to be here. Are we being stalked? Wait, why are we here again? Oh, right of course,' he rushed on speaking, almost urging Tim to pop out of the bushes and scream for him to stop. But, at least he knew one of their names. Al.

Tim studied Al, eyeing everything from his black hair to his worn out, white tennis shoes. Al's blue eyes seemed mysterious yet wise at the same time, and his blank expression told Tim that he was zoning the young teenager out. Al's tanned skin reflected the sun and his shiny black hair was quite long for those of a grown man. 'Eric, I'm sure it's nothing. Just a teen prankster or something.' Hiding in the bushes, Tim almost staggered out at the sound of Al's voice. It was a deep, rumbling sound. A lightning bolt before it strikes.

Before Tim knew it, he felt a firm hand on his shoulder, and let out a small cry of horror for he didn't know what was to happen next. It was Al.

'Who are you and what are you doing here? How long have you been following us? What is your name? Ooh, ooh, ooooh. Is it Eric?' the hyper teenager blabbered on and on, a winding road that never seemed to end. Constantly Tim attempted to interrupt him until finally...

'Eric, shut up,' Al said irritably. Finally, Eric zipped up his portal of flowing words. Tim cleared his throat. 'I—I came to sign up for...um...for the military?' Tim said, his statement sounding like a question. By the expression on his face, Tim could tell that even Eric wasn't buying it. He quickly rushed to cover up his flop. 'I was w-wondering if you young g-gentlemen could help me find directions. I moved here from...' *Think, think, think. What is Macey always mentioning after history class?* 'I'm coming from LeRoyale Earth,' he explained. It sounded believable enough.

'Mmhmm. Well you see...,' Eric continued, attempting to sound mature. Finally, Tim snapped.

'Eric, let me speak. I'm human too, you know.' *I did not just say that.* 'I mean, you know. I'm alive. As a BC.' Tim caught a suspicious look across Al's face, but it passed quickly. Suddenly a thought occurred to him. 'What are you doing here?'

For once, Eric was quiet, leaving the answer for Al. Without a blink of an eye, Al answered. 'We're just doing some surveying for a statistics project.' Tim knew he was lying, but he also knew that he himself was doing nothing better. Little did he know, the worst was over.

∾

15

Discovery

'Oh, so that's how it works,' Tim said, attempting to understand—or at least pretending to understand—whatever Al was talking about. Something about 'one president', 'elections', 'military' and 'recommendations'.

'We're here!' Eric blabbered. 'The Presidential Palace, home to the most important BC on Earth...!' Al had no trouble ignoring Eric, probably from all the practice he'd gotten.

'This is the place,' Al said gruffly. 'You want to join the military? You got to get the approval from the President's trust committee first.' Al paused, before asking a question that Tim had feared all along.

'Why do you want to join the military here if you're from LeRoyale Earth?' he asked.

'Um, I agree with your point of view?' Tim tried, remembering what Macey mentioned after some history lesson.

'Point of view?' Al said. 'Our military...' But he was

interrupted by the security guard that stood in front of the main gate of the Presidential complex.

'My name is Mr Sherwood, how can I help you?' the suited, large man said. His remark sounded more like an assertion than a question, filled with arrogance.

'I'm Al. We have a newbie here, Sherwood. Someone who wants to join the army, he says? What do you have for us?' Al was casual, as if he was talking to an old friend. Mr Sherwood appeared to be a bit surprised at his unusual behaviour.

He recovered quickly, though. 'Um, I'll ring up the military recruiting secretary. Go ahead and step inside, Al. He'll meet you out in the lobby.'

Tim was quite impressed by the architecture of the building. The walls were thin and tall, gleaming with a fresh coat of cream paint. Most of the furniture was like gold: same colour and same value. The ladies at the front counters worked quickly and efficiently, all the while managing to keep their perfectly manicured nails in great condition. He tried to hide his awe, just in case it was common to have such elegant rooms. But as Tim eyed the other two out of the corner of his eye, he noted that for once Eric was speechless. Soon, they were interrupted by a gentle voice.

'Hello, somebody called?' a kind looking BC smiled at them. There was a large chance of Tim getting into the military, if the man was as generous as he looked. Tim stepped forward immediately, not hesitating at this chance to enact his plan.

'Hi, I'm Tim. I'm looking for a spot in the military. Any way you can help me out?'

'I'm the one you're looking for. Would you rather get your

interview over with now, or wait for an official appointment to be scheduled?' Tim pondered the question for a moment.

'Let's do it now,' Tim said, trying to sound as confident as possible.

'Alright then. Nice to meet you, Tim. Come on in. I'm Noah.' Tim had expected an even grander office for somebody as important as Noah, but he was shocked to see it was no tidier than his own office. In fact, the two places were so similar, he almost felt at home in this quaint little room. Noah cleared his throat.

'I want you to sit right here in front of the lie detector,' Noah said. 'Now this detector is a very expensive piece of machinery, and will detect a lying tone in your voice. So I encourage you to tell the truth, the whole truth, and nothing but the truth. It's for your own safety.'

Tim gulped. This was definitely the end. He knew nothing about the military's goals, let alone his past life as a 'BC'. Al and Eric were waiting outside, and Tim wasn't sure whether to be thankful that they wouldn't see this side of him, or to be devastated to be left there without help. He sat in his wooden chair, headphones covering his ears to notify him on whether or not the lie detector had found something that denied the truth hidden in his voice. The detector's mouthpiece rested against Tim's lips, and he sat, awaiting the first question.

Tim twitched as Noah's voice boomed through his headphones. 'Where are you from? What brings you here?' Tim thought the question through, wondering what Noah would be looking for. Slowly, he spoke...

'I'm not from here, and I understand that I do not belong

here. I would like to prove myself as an efficient man who can believe in more than what others tell him,' Tim said. He sat back in his chair, relaxed. Maybe this wouldn't be so hard after all. After all, he wasn't exactly lying.

Back on the spaceship, everybody had fled the evacuation room before the BCs had a chance to investigate twice. The humans had started a life in an underground bunker, in a hallway of twenty-four rooms. The hall was meant especially for occasions of the type, complete with a plumbing system and food storage. Their human ancestors had created a few such bunkers on Earth before being chased away from the planet by the BCs.

Meanwhile, Leslie felt like she had cried out all the tears she could, and was starting to wonder if such a small diary entry that was written years ago by a pre-teen should really affect her friendship with the girl she'd loved forever. After all, she would never understand what Macey went through. Leslie had always known her parents were gone. But not being trusted by your close friend? That was hurtful.

Tim had been gone for a couple weeks now, but Leslie knew he was alright; he messaged every week. Taking care of things around the underground bunker was much easier than she thought it would be; everybody stayed quiet. It was as if they were children waiting for their teacher to enter their classroom again. But somehow, Leslie still felt like a leader, for she had been the closest to Tim when they still dwelled in the spaceship.

'Food shortage in room 12,' somebody said through the loudspeaker. The loudspeaker was another convenient add-on. All the demands and commands of any passenger would be spoken through this device and the message would be carried around until it echoed all throughout the hall. Then, anybody who had whatever was needed would reply through the loudspeaker. This way, everybody relied on everybody else. 'I repeat: food shortage in room 12.'

As the conversation between a member in room 12 and a member in room 7 continued, Leslie bustled around busily in her own mini kitchen. Twenty-four rooms weren't enough to hold all of the families that thrived on the spaceship; so many small families were forced to room together. Leslie was a lone wanderer, and nobody there was family to her. Her roommates were plentiful: Seven-year-old twins (one male, and one female) and one widowed mother. The mother, who was named Mrs Anderson, had alternating cooking shifts that she shared with Leslie. Today, of course, it was Leslie's turn. Quite frankly, Leslie was glad, for Mrs Anderson was not the best cook one could ask for.

'Mrs Anderson! Little Andersons! Dinner's ready!' Leslie always had trouble remembering the twins' names: Nellie and Frankie. She just referred to them as the Little Andersons.

'Oh, oh dear me,' Mrs Anderson mumbled under her breath while she felt around her bedside table for her glasses. The rooms in which everybody dwelled were not at all big and luxurious. Everybody could see everybody else, whether you were cooking, working, or sleeping. It was all the same.

The kitchen was a tiny, counter bordered rectangle that

held all the necessities: a refrigerator, a microwave, a sink, and an oven. There weren't really bedrooms, just two bunk beds lined up against the sides of the walls, and one big desk in the centre of the room. It wasn't any different than what an average hotel room would be like back in 2030.

'What's for dinner?' one of the excited twins chattered continuously, ignoring the answer to her question.

'Meat loaf,' the other twin said with a face. 'What a classic.'

'Meat loaf's good, especially when Leslie makes it.' Nellie shot back.

'Nuh-uh,' Frankie replied, sticking his tongue out.

'Yuh-huh.'

'It's not delicious at all.'

'Yes it is!' The arguing seemed like it would never end and Leslie just rolled her eyes as she served herself a small portion of dinner.

'Oh, children, please do stop squabbling,' Mrs Anderson said in her what they understood as an old British accent. She was so quaint, with her way of speaking, the way she dressed, and the way she dealt with situations like these. 'Your dear mother is quite tired. Oh, and Frankie, please be quiet and eat your meat loaf like a good little boy. Spare me from having to walk you through this conversation again.' Mrs Anderson seemed like she was talking to herself now, mumbling under her breath until nobody bothered to listen anymore.

Leslie hunched over her paper plate and let her golden locks shut the complicated world out for another half hour. While devouring her chewy meat, Leslie let her thoughts wander again. She couldn't wait for Monday to roll around again;

that's when she'd receive Tim's progress report. It'd been three days since her last one; it was only Thursday. But she could wait however many days it would take until Macey was safe in her arms again.

'Leslie, dear, just leave your dirty plates on the table, I'll clear it all up in a moment,' said Mrs Anderson, quite fraily. On a regular basis, Leslie would deny the offer and clean up herself, but at the moment, she had to figure out what she was feeling and sort out her crazy thoughts. Absentmindedly, Leslie nodded her head.

'Thank you Mrs Anderson,' she replied, before hopping onto her top bunk and sliding out her communicator to check her messages. Her message queue was mostly empty since Macey left, because the two exchanged short messages all the time. She assumed Macey had lost all contact with her, but she was wrong. Sitting in her message queue as the only unread item lay a letter from Macey. Leslie pondered on whether or not to open it for a while, deciding what she should expect and how she should react. But when she finally mustered the courage to open it, she did not at all see what she had anticipated.

Dear Leslie,

I've missed you a lot lately, how have you been? Well, if you ask me, I've had the journey of a lifetime. When the BCs took me away, I stayed for weeks inside something called the Presidential Palace. Sure, it was luxurious, but I'll never go back there again.

While I was there, a nearby history museum opened up an exhibit just for me. It was called 'The Human'.

Isn't that crazy? Well, over there I met this boy, his name's Dylan. Instantly, we had some connection. A few days later, he came back to the Presidential Palace and tried to bust me out! It worked, with the help of one of my BC friends, Emma.

Dylan and I went through a lot together, and finally, he agreed to take me to Forbidden Earth, where our spaceship had landed. We couldn't find you there! So, we decided to settle down. I'm now a mother of two kids, Kimberly and Logan. They're so cute! Now, enough about me. I have one question for you. Where in the universe are you? Please reply soon, I can't wait to see you.

Love,
Macey

Leslie held her breath for a moment. She had finally read Macey's words. She knew Macey was alright; that she wasn't being tortured. She looked at the date it was sent. *Tuesday,* it read. It'd been only two days since Macey had sent the message. That couldn't be bad, could it?

But one thing haunted Leslie. Macey had broken out, and suddenly Leslie had no clue if anything Tim had done was worth anything at all. She had to inform Tim about her discovery as soon as possible. But first, she'd write back to Macey. Leslie clicked on 'Reply', wishing with all her heart that everything would work out in the end. The sound of her fingers on the screen seemed louder than ever as she typed.

Dear Macey,

I'm so glad you're alright! This Dylan of yours seems nice, but are you sure he's keeping you safe? He is, after all, a BC.

We took off when you were captured; I'm so sorry. But, we're on Earth again and Tim has gone on a quest to find you. Now, he's somewhere in the middle of a city. Possibly at the Presidential Palace. I'll definitely let him know you're safe. I know he is; I get his progress reports weekly. I'll make sure I attach them to this message. Everything's just so complicated now. Keep in touch, though. I miss you and I hope everything works out.

Lots of love,
Leslie

Leslie made sure to keep away from anything personal; she'd save that for when the two were face to face. Next, she messaged Tim. She wrote all about how Macey was alright, how Macey had a BC boyfriend, and how Tim had to find Macey on his way back.

Leslie sighed with discontent. She was so confused. What was going to happen? Would she ever see her dear friends again? At this point of time, she was even more worried than she was in the beginning, when Macey had left them.

Leslie fought the urge to message Macey again, to keep on chatting with her and exchanging details about everything. But she just sighed, powered down her messaging system and slid it back into its constant place in between her mattresses.

'Oh, Macey,' she said, one tear sliding down her cheek. 'How much longer until I can hold you in my arms? I miss you so much.' Leslie felt a few tears wet her t-shirt, but she didn't care. Finally, she added three more, meaningful words to her prayer. 'I love you.'

16

What do I do?

'Dylan, what do you need? Should I get you...um...a cough drop? Do you need water? Oh, please speak to me!' Macey cried desperately. 'I need you! I can't do this alone...'

Dylan lay groaning on the bed through pain, guilt, and sorrow. 'Macey, I'm fine. Go check on the kids. I'm sure they need something,' he responded before turning over in his bed and falling asleep again. It was hard to fall asleep at all with his swollen arm, which was starting to puff out abnormally, but it was the only way to keep the pain away.

'Oh, alright. I hate to do this to you, Dylan. Anytime you need something, just give me a holler,' Macey whispered into his ear. That was the last thing she said before walking out and leaving Dylan on the bed, all alone.

Macey had only been playing with Logan, who was able to talk now, for a couple of minutes before hearing a sharp cry of pain come from Dylan's bedroom.

'Macey!' he cried. 'Oh, hurry! The pain is killing me!' Dylan yelled again. Macey felt like she had never run faster in her life.

'Dylan! Oh, just hang in there. I'm on my way!' Macey shouted. When she arrived next to Dylan's bed, she felt like she'd never seen anybody in more pain.

'Macey, this is the maximum. There's no way you can ever cure me, I've gone too far,' he said in between coughs. Macey was nodding her head 'no'.

'Well, then you have to let me call the BCs in Northern Earth. And there's no way you can stop me!' Macey had the phone held up to her ear. She was right; there was no stopping her now. She was willing to risk her freedom to save Dylan's life.

But just because Macey was bold enough to make the first move, it didn't mean that she was any less nervous. She bit her lip as she heard the 'bring' sound ring in her ear.

'Hello, what's your emergency?' a kind female voice asked over the globe phone. *She's only kind because she doesn't know who I am,* Macey thought bitterly. She didn't have to try to disguise her voice; no one would recognise her. It'd been almost two years.

'Hi. I have an injured BC here. He, um, was stung by a bee. Our teleporter had some sort of malfunction, and we ended up in Forbidden Earth. How fast can you get here?' Macey was surprised at how smoothly she spoke. Quick, and to the point.

'I'm sorry to hear that, but it may be too late. How long has he had this sting?' the woman over the phone said. Suddenly, her voice sounded crude and harsh to Macey. Macey's heart skipped a beat.

'Too late? Oh, no, no, it's not too late, is it? Just get here as fast as you can!' Macey tried to keep calm. But this much was crossing the line. She tried to relax by thinking about how BCs could teleport to her location in a number of seconds.

'Alright, but since you have no exact location, it'll be hard to pinpoint you. Is it okay if I install a tracking device in your phone right now? It can be done in a couple of minutes,' she said. *Wow,* Macey thought. *Technology really has gotten better.* It was also not as safe. Say they somehow found out that she was the human? Then she'd have to abandon her phone, and that seemed out of the question with all the complications that somehow strangled themselves into her life. *I'd also lose communication with Leslie,* she pointed out to herself, remembering how she'd figured out how to send messages to Leslie from her phone across communication matrices. But Macey had no choice.

'That'd be great,' she finally sighed. She heard a small click before music started playing into her ear. She had been put on hold.

After a minute or so, the tinkling voice spoke again. 'Installation is complete. We will be there in less than a minute.'

'Oh. Thank you so much, I don't...' but before Macey could finish, she was interrupted by a sudden burst of dust, clouding her face until she felt like she could only breathe as well as Dylan could.

'We're here! Where's the emergency?' a different voice called. The voice still belonged to a female, but this time, she was tough-sounding. When the woman showed the back of her head, Macey was taken aback by shock.

'Emma? Is that you?' she said. The reddish-brown hair

whipped back quickly, revealing none other than the woman that helped her escape.

'Oh my. Macey? This isn't happening. That can't be you. I'm imagining this,' Emma started to talk to herself. When she finally pulled herself together, she looked up.

'Macey, we'll have our reunion later,' Emma paused. 'Oh no. The BC you were talking about was Dylan, wasn't it?' Solemnly, Macey closed her eyes and nodded, but by the time she opened them again, Emma was gone, rushing towards the little hut on the shore.

'Emma, be careful! You can get sick too!' Macey shouted behind her. But Emma, using her supersonic speed, had already entered the hut.

'Dylan!' she called. But she didn't need to hear a reply, for Dylan's moaning had filled up the whole house. 'Dylan, I'm here. Come on. There you go.'

Macey could only hear Emma's voice from a distance; she was too shocked, and could not run nearly as fast as a BC. By the time she reached the entrance to Dylan's room, Emma was already on her way out, with Dylan limp in her arms.

'Emma! Wait up!' she screamed, panting as she tried to keep up. Even when Emma was carrying all of Dylan's weight, she was still at least five times faster than Macey. Thankfully, Emma decided Dylan could spare a couple seconds in order to make sure Macey wasn't left behind.

'Thanks,' Macey let out a long breath after finally hopping into the back seat of the teleporter. Dylan lay moaning in the first seat, mumbling words like 'April' and 'sorry'. Macey blinked, and in that split second, she found herself in front of a white building with a red sign reading 'Emergency Room'.

'Is it that bad?' Macey mumbled under her breath, following Emma, who was bearing Dylan's weight again. Before entering the emergency room, Emma laid Dylan down on a bench and pulled out a walkie-talkie.

'We have a bee sting at the entrance. Clear out a room, he only has a few minutes. Over,' she said, eyeing Dylan's arm again.

'Got it. Over,' a male voice replied through her walkie-talkie. Emma carried Dylan inside the ER just in time to see a man in a white coat rushing their way. It was the doctor. He was followed by a crew of three bustling nurses, who were lifting Dylan's body into a rolling bed. Meanwhile, the white-suited man yelled frantically.

'Injection #27! No, scratch that. Hand me #46!' he shouted again. By the time he had a needle in his hand, Dylan had been pushed into a room and had been connected to a heart rate monitor. It beeped slowly, which was bad news. The nurses polished Dylan's arm with some sort of oil, and the doctor was just about to inject him with his needle before Emma whispered to Macey...

'Macey, it's required that you and your two children are put under observation to check if any harm has been done. You're on the top wanted list though. You have been since I helped you escape. And now you're back here again. We better pray they don't discover your secret. I'm really sorry,' she said, pulling Macey by the arm and out the door. *Great.* Macey thought. *Another thing to worry about.*

'Wait, where are the kids?' Macey said, her eyes opening

wide. She didn't remember them ever entering the teleporter.

'Don't worry, we have it under control. They've already been put under observation. Right in here,' Emma said, still whispering. She gestured towards an open elevator, and Macey stepped in. The elevator was not anything special. Probably something that could be easily built on the spaceship.

'Okay,' Macey shakily replied. Her limbs shook like an avalanche about to tumble after a heavy snow storm. Finally, she heard the *ding* of the elevator door.

'Destination reached: Observation Room,' the robotic, monotone voice said. As Macey stepped out of the elevator, dozens of eyes glazed over her every move. She was behind glass, and all these eyes were staring at her through the window. Somehow, Emma had reached the other side as well, and was watching too. But Macey knew she was watching for a different reason.

The kids were in the observation room, just as Emma had promised, and Macey held them tightly. *Please, keep my secret safe.* Macey prayed. But she knew there was a slim chance of her leaving the room undiscovered.

'One unread message,' Tim's messaging pad beeped from across the table. Tim wondered who could be messaging him at this time. Only Leslie had been messaging him lately, and that was only when she responded to his progress reports every Monday. But if Leslie was contacting him now, it was probably important. But it was horrible timing as well; he was still in the middle of Noah's interview. He'd done okay so far. Tim had managed not to lie, but at the same time he gave reasonable answers.

'One more question, and you're good to go. You came in at the right time, we're short on military officials,' Noah sighed. 'So, do you have a child or wife who may interfere with your performance in the military?'

Tim gulped. What was he supposed to say now? There was no way out of this but to tell the truth. But not the whole truth, for sure. 'My wife has passed away,' Tim kept it simple, trying not to get into detail about how, for he didn't know how difficult it was for a BC to die. 'And my daughter is not with me right now. She, uh, was kidnapped.' Tim added, realising what he said was true. He was careful not to mention that his military application had everything to do with his daughter. Tim noticed a questioning look in Noah's eyes which was replaced with indifference soon after. 'Welcome to the army, Tim Johnson. I hope you mean what you say. I will send you your approval seal within the next week. Good luck, and have fun. You are dismissed,' Noah said, turning his chair towards his desk as if Tim was already gone. In a hurry, Tim grabbed his messaging pad and jolted out of the door.

As soon as he had reached the lobby, Tim pulled into the nearest chair to open up his message box. 'One unread message,' the pad beeped again.

'I know, I know,' Tim mumbled. He cursed under his breath when he realized he had to enter his password. *This is going to take forever* he thought, groaning out load. When he had finally overcome all his obstacles, he clicked quickly on the

'Message box' button. All of his unread messages stood out, whiter than the ones he'd already read. Tim gulped when he saw that his latest message was from Leslie. He opened it, apprehensive about what it will say. Slowly he read:

Dear Tim,

You'll never guess what I just discovered. Macey is alright! In fact, she's near the location where we last landed our spaceship. You have to come back, and fast! Come up with an excuse, and once you are back we can go and look for Macey. But it might be hard, because you'll never guess what else. She is married to a BC now and they have two children, one boy and one girl. I just don't know what to think any more. Help me out Tim!

Can't wait to see you again,

Leslie

Tim re-read it a couple of times, not believing what he read. *This is just great,* he thought. *I just told Noah that no matter what, Macey wouldn't affect my efficiency in the army.* It would've been a lot easier if he read the message before answering Noah's last question. But it was a good thing he hadn't left the Presidential Palace yet. Tim was left only with one option: to consult Noah on his change of plans.

'This is going to be hard,' he told himself. But at the same time, another voice in his head was saying, 'Your daughter is more important than Noah's opinion of you.' Finally, Tim knocked on Noah's door. His knock was slow and suspicious, though, like a stranger waiting to be accepted into a house after a storm.

'Come in,' Noah's muffled voice called through the door. 'Why, hello Tim. Is something wrong?' Noah asked as Tim stepped through the door.

'Yes, there is something wrong. I'm sorry, but I can't take my being accepted into the army,' Tim sighed. *This is going well,* he thought. *Just keep away from the truth, keep away from the...*

'Well, why ever not?' Noah asked, smiling goofily as if it was a joke.

'Um, my daughter has been found,' he said guiltily. So much for keeping away from the truth. Noah's face darkened immediately.

'I see you didn't mean what you said,' Noah stiffened. 'It's good you came in. You didn't tell the whole truth, and I see that you would've been a disgrace to our army. Don't bother coming back,' Noah said in a monotone, turning his chair. It seemed as if the cheery, goofy Noah had been replaced by a much crueller one. Tim felt a pang of guilt echo through the pit of his stomach.

'Noah, you don't understand,' he frowned. 'Have you ever lost a child? Do you know how much it hurts?' As soon as the words slipped from his mouth, he regretted them. Of course BC's wouldn't know; they didn't feel too much emotion.

But apparently, Noah did. His face melted back into its normal condition as his eyes widened sympathetically. 'Tim, it's alright. You're right. I don't understand, and I hope I never do. Go now, see your daughter. You are dismissed.'

Tim walked out without saying another word, praying that Noah wouldn't turn around again and ruin his Mr Nice-Guy image. 'Whew,' Tim ran his hand across his forehead. One down, two to go. Eric and Al. Before heading outside again, Tim grabbed his message pad from the chair.

Eric and Al were both waiting outside the door, seated on the bench opposite the main entrance. 'How'd you do?' Al asked in his normal, deep voice. Tim looked down guiltily at his shoes when he answered.

'I made it,' he said. Al looked worried for a second.

'Then why are you so upset?' he furrowed his brow. Tim sighed.

'Guys, I've been keeping a secret from you.'

'No kidding,' Al laughed. But although Al knew Tim was keeping a secret, he had no idea how crazy it was. That Tim was human, and the only reason he was on Earth was because his daughter had been kidnapped over a year ago. But, not for the first time, Tim hid the whole truth.

'I...um...my daughter was kidnapped around two years ago, and she has been found. By one of her close friends, I mean. I have to go back and meet her. She's had a hard time, these two years,' Tim finally relaxed his shoulders. His excuse wasn't perfect, but at least it was believable.

Eric looked worried, and raised his head to speak. 'Mr Johnson, why would a BC kidnap your daughter? We have nothing against each other. Plus, we don't have much emotion, like those stupid humans, so we can't exactly hold grudges.'

Tim's face paled. 'It's different. I don't really have time to explain it right now,' Tim said hurriedly. 'Would it bother you too much if I used your teleporter again?'

Eric looked unsure, but Al seemed willing to help. 'Sure

thing,' Al said. 'Just send it back here when you're done.'

'Thank you so, so much,' Tim sighed, relieved to have met Al, who had been such a huge help from the start. 'And I'll definitely send it back,' Tim added in a hurry. *If I can figure out how to use the freaking thing,* he swore under his breath. 'Thanks again. For everything,' Tim smiled. Contentedly, he sighed. He knew that whatever information he had given the BCs wasn't enough, but who cared? *As long as I get away with it,* Tim told himself, seating himself in the driver's seat of Al's teleporter. It was quite old looking—white and rusty. But Tim didn't care, as long as it was his ticket to home, sweet home.

'Let's figure this baby out,' Tim smiled pushing the button that read 'Power'. 'This is going to be fun,' Tim laughed out loud, feeling like the main hero out of one of his action movies. Immediately, the teleporter powered up, rumbling beneath his feet. The screen in front of him lit up, making his face glow with colour.

'Where would you like to travel today?' the screen seemed to ask, revealing a list of top visited places. Of course, none of them read his destination. So instead, Tim typed 'Forbidden Earth' into the search engine.

'Are you sure you would like to visit Forbidden Earth?' the screen asked again. This time, the screen glowed with two colours: green and red. The green button read 'No', while the red button read 'Yes'. *It can't be that bad,* Tim said, finally realising that Forbidden Earth was really frowned upon.

'For Macey!' he shouted, before pressing 'Yes' and feeling the cold wind burn his face with glee.

17

---❧---

Trouble in Northern Earth

'It's okay Logan, it's okay. I'm right here,' Macey comforted the crying baby, who was bringing his twin sister to tears as well.

'Mommy, when we see Daddy?' Kimberly cried, one tear dribbling down her pale cheek. She'd just learned how to connect words and make sentences, but she wasn't a pro at it.

Confidence is the key, Macey told herself. *If I'm okay, the kids will be okay.* She raised her chin, facing the BCs who were scribbling down notes and watching her every move.

'When will I be released?' she asked, her confidence level pumping at an extraordinary degree. *Don't be overconfident,* she told herself. *That'll just ruin everything.* A BC spoke to her through his microphone, the only thing she could hear in the silence of the room.

'You will be released when we have connected your and Dylan's DNAs to your children's to check your relationship, and how his sickness may have carried on to you and/or your children.' With a nod of his head, the BC turned his head back to his notes. This time, a female stepped forward to the microphone.

'Please proceed to the DNA testing lab,' she said. A thought suddenly occurred to Macey. What sort of DNA did BCs have? How different would it be from human DNA? After all, the BCs had a bit modified form of human cells, according to her scientific history books. If she questioned their procedures, perhaps Macey would appear human.

The BC that had spoken to her first walked into the observation room and lifted Logan out of his seat. He was followed by graceful Emma, who then lifted Kimberly out of her seat, who had been placed on the right of Logan. Both of them kicked and screamed at the action of being taken away from their dear mother, who followed in a hurry, trying to get them to feel at ease.

'W-what exactly is going to happen in here?' Macey stuttered, bustling after the two BCs.

'Oh, it's quite simple, really,' the male BC said. His name tag read 'Mr Applewood'. *It's not like I'd bother to call him by his last name. More like Mr I'm-going-to-uncover-all-your-secrets. I.G.T.U.A.Y.S. for short. Hmm…Not that easy to remember.*

Mr Applewood kept talking. 'All you have to do is sit down in this special chair, while we do all the work!' he said, in one of those phony voices that are used when talking to a three year old. When he wasn't looking, Macey rolled her eyes. She asked to carry her own children. Mr Applewood denied her plea, but at least Emma let her hold Kimberly.

'Don't worry, it'll be alright,' she told the pair of big, blue eyes that stared up at her. Macey wasn't even convinced herself. Kimberly's puppy eyes grew wider as she planted a small kiss on her mom's cheek.

'I love you, mommy,' she said, in her baby-like accent, making it sound more like *I dub wu, wommy*.

'I love you too, Kim,' Macey whispered. 'Now you just be a good little girl while this nice young man runs tests on you,' she sneered, talking more to herself now. Nice? That man was ripping her life apart. But she knew he didn't mean to. And how would you tell somebody nicely that somebody's about to run tests on them? You wouldn't. That's how.

'Good luck, Macey,' Emma whispered again. 'I really didn't expect this. If you make it out of this alive, we'll have a little celebration,' she laughed, hoping to make the mood lighter. It was a failed attempt.

Macey ended the conversation with a simple 'Mmhmm'. She used a death glare to eye Mr Applewood. He didn't seem to think the least of it, flipping switches and pushing buttons while Macey remained seated—as a hopeless being who was about to be tested on.

Suddenly Macey felt it. It came fast, but it didn't leave nearly as quickly. It was a gnawing feeling at the pit of her stomach, crawling up till her throat, about to emerge in a silent, mouthed cry of worry. Fear. That's what it was.

'I can't do this,' she whispered to herself. Fear was so powerful. But Macey remained confident. Maybe they wouldn't find anything out of the ordinary.

'Please remain seated in the DNA testing chair,' another raspy voice said. A new person waited in front of the glass this time. Macey guessed that DNA was this woman's area of expertise.

'Nah nahnahnahnah,' Macey imitated, scrunching up her nose. She was glad the glass was mostly soundproof. 'This isn't going to hurt, is it?' she asked. This time she was loud enough so that Mrs Raspy-Voice could hear her.

'No, not at all,' she pulled some more words out of the back of her throat. 'There,' she said. Suddenly, a huge light filled the room, but it dimmed almost instantly. 'All done! Now I'm sending a copy of the test to some professionals to look it over. In the mean time, you can visit your loved ones. If you wish, we can care for your children while you go. You can also take them with you.'

'I think I'll take them with me. Our family has a few traditions we like to share. I'd like to cherish the moment,' Macey muttered. BCs didn't feel emotion. How unfortunate. But on second thought, perhaps they could learn. After all, Dylan showed an obvious affection for Macey and the kids.

Immediately, the phone next to the raspy-voiced woman's clipboard blared. *Bringg! Bringg!* 'The professionals, already...?' she asked herself, trying to understand. 'Hello?' she answered unsurely. The phone was on speaker mode and loud enough for Macey to catch a few words.

'We encountered an error; the data you sent us was surprising. It does not seem like BC DNA. Please report to room 14A immediately.'

'A-alright. What could've gone wrong? I mean, the BC seems perfectly nor...' the doctor couldn't finish her sentence. When she looked up to study the 'normal BC', she saw an 'emotional human' that seemed visibly worried.

'I can't do this,' she was whispering. Macey knew she was being a dead give away, given that BCs didn't feel too much emotion. But she tried to cover it up as far as covering it up could go. It wasn't a dam to stop the river, but at least it was a rowboat to get across.

'I need to see Dylan,' she whimpered, putting her good acting skills to use.

'Alright, dear. Just go right ahead. Room 12B. I'll return shortly.' Apparently, the doctor thought nothing of Macey's breakdown. To her, a job was more important at the moment. Before Macey could respond, the nervous female was already fleeting up the stairs to room 14A. It was time for Macey to move on as well.

'Come on Logan. Kimberly, let's go see Daddy. See, that wasn't so bad, was it?' Macey said, calmer now. Her attitude seemed to calm down the two jabbering babies as well. They spoke words of happiness, and rejoiced at the ringing tone of Macey's voice. But they stopped abruptly.

'Is da-ddy oh-kay?' Logan asked. His word usage and pronunciation was still iffy.

'Yes, the doctors said he'd be fine.' But that's just something doctors always say. 'Let's go now, before his caretakers shut down his room for the night.' Macey proceeded to the left side of the DNA testing lab, and pushed the soundless door open.

'Room 12B, room 12B,' Macey reminded herself repeatedly. Soon, her children chorused with her as well.

'Room 12B, room 12B,' they gurgled, waddling along as Macey shoved her finger into the elevator button with the arrow pointing upwards. 'Going up!' Logan giggled, feeling utterly clever with his usage of the word 'going'.

When the three of them had reached floor 'B', they scattered and started searching for Room 12. Well, partially scattered anyway, Macey wouldn't let the kids out of her sight. After all, they couldn't really tell numbers apart. What was the use?

'Room 12B!' Macey shouted, catching a glimpse of the silver characters engraved into the blue door. As a reflex, Macey burst into the room without thinking twice.

'Dylan!' she cried.

'Daddy!' yelled Logan.

'Papa,' whimpered Kimberly. All three of them could tell by Dylan's blank expression and rolled up eyes that he did not hear any of them. And all three of them prayed that their dearest Dylan was alive.

∾

'Leslie! Macey!' Tim yelled with glee, it occurring to him that both his loved ones were within a few miles radius from where he stood. Or so he thought.

Soon enough, he spotted the wrecked spaceship and glanced around the fuming sight to double check that no more BCs were investigating the place. After he granted himself a clear signal, he rushed to the underground bunker where he knew his people were.

With a thud, he dropped into the hallway and started looking for Leslie's room. 'Leslie? Mrs Anderson?' he called, knowing that Mrs Anderson and her two children were Leslie's roommates.

'Yes?' somebody finally responded, leaving a tinkling sound echoing throughout the narrow hall. It was none other than the gorgeous young girl that had stayed with Tim even while he was gone. Leslie's locks tumbled down her slim neck and cascaded right past her shoulders. She seemed to have grown taller, and her face looked more mature. Even her eyes seemed larger, and more intelligent.

'I'm back,' Tim whispered, a soft smile touching his lips. The two family members embraced, as if they hadn't seen each other in a long time.

'I have to tell you something about Macey,' Leslie said, keeping her voice hushed as well. Tim loosened his grip and braced himself for whatever Leslie had to tell him. 'I'm really sorry about this, but I just found out that Macey is no longer in Forbidden Earth. Macey's BC husband got sick. Oh, his name's Dylan by the way. Macey messaged me saying how much she cared for him, and that she had sent herself up to Northern Earth to be with Dylan while they take care of him in the hospital.'

Now, Tim was angry. 'Is she crazy? They're going to discover her secret! How will we ever get her out of this mess...?' he sighed at the last bit.

'Tim, don't waste your time. Macey made that decision. We just have to wait and see what happens.'

'I guess you're right,' Tim said, shutting his eyes. He quickly opened them again. This time he was more cheerful, as if he had suddenly learned to live in the present. 'I'm hungry,' he said in a tired tone.

'So what?' Leslie joked, continuing on his streak.

'So, what's cooking?' he joked. Leslie laughed along with him as she led him into her room to eat leftover meat loaf.

'Hi! Mrs Anderson!' he said with a flick of his two front fingers, in the form of a salute. 'Oh, why hello, Frankie. Nellie,' he smiled. It seemed like life for the next few weeks wouldn't be so bad, after all.

❧

Meanwhile, at the Northern Earth Medical Center, Macey was bawling, along with her sobbing kids. 'Oh, Dylan, please speak to me!'

'Papa, Dada!' the kids chorused together. Finally, one crusted eye of Dylan's peeled upwards.

'Eh?' he asked.

'Oh my god, thank goodness, you're alive!' Macey cried, tilting her chin towards heaven as if to thank her own personal God. On top of that, Logan and Kimberly joined hands and stopped their crying immediately. But their happy, to-be-cherished moment was ruined when somebody spoke sharply through the loudspeaker system.

'Macey Johnson, report to the front desk as soon as possible,' the harsh tone said, stressing the last four words. By the time Macey looked back at Dylan, both his eyes were open.

'You can't go, they've most likely discovered your secret,' he said weakly.

'But I have to,' Macey smiled reassuringly, giving Dylan's

hand a quick squeeze before gently pushing Logan, Kim, and herself through the door.

Once the family reached the front desk on Floor A, Macey thought that she couldn't have been put under any more pressure. Stern faces stared at her from every angle, and everybody seemed to hold a sudden grudge against her.

'Macey Johnson, I'm afraid it has come to our attention that you've been keeping a secret from us, and you are a major threat to the population of BCs,' the main woman behind the desk said. This time, even the BCs that weren't staring at her rudely beforehand stared with interest. The suspense in the room was too much to handle. *Play dumb*, Macey told herself.

'What's so secretive about a normal BC coming to visit a loved one?' she asked smoothly. *Good job*, she congratulated herself.

Now, the woman at the front desk was annoyed. She rolled her eyes and gritted her teeth. 'One problem,' she said sarcastically. 'You're not a normal BC. You're a human.' Suddenly everybody within earshot gasped.

Macey acted shocked too. But that's the thing, she wasn't shocked. Not at all. 'What proof do you have of that nonsense?' she sneered, challenging her opponent.

'Your DNA, there was an error found while processing it. You and your kids as well, although they seemed only half human. Which means...' she paused for dramatic effect. 'You've been in a close relationship with a BC. Our best guess would be Dylan. He will be pressed with criminal charges, and the President has been notified of your presence on Earth. He has also been informed that you are the same woman who had escaped unexpectedly from the Presidential place.' This time, Macey didn't act. Her face paled.

'What? N-no, you can't do that. Can you?' she seemed to question herself.

'I'm sorry ma'am. Your boyfriend will be taken care of, though, since he is a BC. We will not present any physical harm to him, and will not inform him of our discovery, just in case he's not aware of it, until he recovers.' Out of nowhere, security appeared, lifting Macey up by her arms. Almost like a déjà vu moment. It was the exact same way she had been captured a while ago.

'But he knows! He knows I'm...human! Please, tell him you've...found me!' Her pleas seemed stupid, making her feel like a llama that had just been discovered in a group of fine mustangs.

'I'm sorry, Macey. But us informing him will only make him panic, resulting in an upsetting delay in his recovey,' the lady smiled, seeming pleased with herself for making such an important announcement. 'Oh, and you and your children will be in for a questions and answers session with the President tomorrow,' she added.

∽

18

·⚬⚬⚬·

Prayer

'Welcome ladies and BCs, to the event of a lifetime,' a chubby man with blonde hair smiled into the camera. 'Today, we are hosting a rare event. A human, real as I am, was found in the Northern Earth Medical Center, and has been summoned here to take part in a questions and answers session,' he said, nodding his head this time, his smile growing bigger. 'The story continues, just tune in to News at 7 with Amy Bell and Jared Smith.' The camera backed off and the screen of viewers all around Earth faded to black for the commercial break. Macey watched all the production magic happen, for she was backstage, just waiting for the session to begin.

It wasn't as if she had come by choice. She could've been held in jail for the rest of her life if she didn't participate in this 'event of a lifetime'. After all, she was the celebrity guest.

'Come on,' a BC with crazy, blue hair hurried Macey along. 'Time for your final coating of makeup,' she whispered.

Even though the BCs weren't trying to make Macey look

good, they still put her through all the hair and makeup sessions that a real celebrity would have to go through. As the blue-haired woman summoned her through the dressing room, where the co-hosts were getting ready, and the hair designing room, Macey didn't feel so upset after all. She was living the life of a celebrity.

As they neared the makeup artist's trailer, Macey held her breath. The lady was short and plump. Well, of BC women she wasn't the nicest BC either.

'Sit,' she grunted, gesturing towards a leathery chair placed in front of a mirror. Macey obeyed without question and out of the corner of her eye, she watched the blue-haired woman leave. She waited while her makeup artist touched up her cheekbones with blush, and coated her puckered lips in a shiny sheet of gloss. For the first time, Macey saw her smile. *She must really love her job,* Macey thought.

'So, this must be really scary for you, huh?' the woman said. *So, this must be really awkward for you, huh?* Macey snapped back bitterly in her head. She would never say such a thing out loud. Instead, she said...

'Yeah, I feel like an alien.'

'Because you are an alien,' the makeup artist replied. Her voice was coated in a thick, French accent that made everything about her seem so much more sophisticated.

'Touché,' Macey agreed. The makeup lady wasn't that bad of company. But their time together was almost up. With a glance at her wrist watch, Macey noted that there were only ten minutes left before Macey would be live before BCs all over the world.

'You look beautiful,' the woman grinned, admiring her work. 'Well, for a human at least.'

'Thanks.' Macey's eyes grew wide when she caught a glimpse of herself in the mirror. 'There's no way that's me.'

'Oh, but it is.' The woman smiled, her accent mesmerizing Macey once again. 'But lose the watch. Doesn't it clash with the gorgeous white dress the designers picked out for you?' she added with a frown.

'Fine,' Macey mumbled, undoing the golden piece of metal that circled her wrist. The watch felt cold in her hands as Macey clutched it in her tight grasp.

'Charlotte, send the human over to the set. We're filming in five,' a male voice spoke through a speaker. Macey guessed this man was the same man who was hosting the show.

'Alright, that's your cue,' the lady—Charlotte bustled Macey out her trailer. 'Oh, and good luck,' she poked her head through the almost shut door before slamming it closed in Macey's face.

'Alright then,' Macey said, cocking her head to one side. She looked completely baffled. But her time would be taken up trying to find her way back to the stage. The whole place was so big; it was a huge hole that placed you anywhere it pleased. 'Where am I?' Macey frowned.

Slowly, she retraced her steps, trying to recall all the places she went to with the blue-haired woman. 'Ah, here we are,' she sighed with discontent. She saw the huge letters reading SET 3, the location of the production of her broadcast show. 'Another place where I can be used for the BC's entertainment.' Macey walked in and was hit with awe, for the second time since she came on set. She was seeing the exact same room—

the filming room—but seeing it twice didn't wear its beauty.

The filming room was like a living room out of a magazine. A large sofa with full-looking pillows on it rested in the center, with two chairs—made of the same material—standing perpendicular on both sides of it. The chairs and sofa were a light beige colour, and went well with the rest of the décor colour scheme. Most of the decorations were red, as well as the pillows that lined the sofa. Thick red garlands swirled the walls and worked alongside abstract paintings to complete the whole 'I'm on global prime time broadcast' kind of attitude.

'Welcome to the *Griffin Show*! I'm James Griffin, and we're here with Macey Johnson, a live human, for a question and answers session. She's here with her two children, Logan and Kimberly, who appear to be only half human. Now, please give a round of applause for…Macey Johnson!'

Macey walked out from behind the curtain and onto the stage, smiling and waving. She wasn't sure whether to look upset because she had been captured or happy because she was on live global broadcast. 'Thank you for having me,' she smiled into James's microphone. Immediately, she regretted the statement. She shouldn't be grateful at all.

'Well, actually, I feel like I should be thanking you,' James said, faking another cheesy smile. 'Now, take a seat here,' he said, gesturing towards one of the beige sofas. 'Logan! Kimberly! Come join your mommy,' he nodded in the direction of the two kids coming to join Macey. At that moment, there was a huge difference between what Macey was doing, and what Macey wanted to be doing. She was sitting on the couch with a brick wall as a face. She wanted to give both her kids a hug and make sure they were safe.

'Hey there,' she said, instead, through a tight smile. The kids smiled, relief filling their eyes, as if they were happy to finally see a connection to their happy days.

'Hi Mommy,' Logan said, his eyes crinkling with joy. James cleared his throat, snapping the other three back to reality.

'So, Logan, what do you remember about where you lived?' he asked.

'You can't ask my kids for private information,' Macey hissed, angry now.

'Watch me,' he mouthed, so viewers couldn't hear his rude comment. Then, he spoke out loud. 'Did you have a nice house? Or did your Mommy deprive you of all that?' Macey made a face. This man was ruining her kids.

'Daddy built our house on the beach,' Logan smiled. 'I love it there. You can hear the white waves crashing against the sand and the seagulls cawing in the sky, and...' Logan couldn't finish. But his response was enough to throw James back in surprise. He was expecting something trashy that would ruin Macey's reputation as a human.

'Yes, well that's very nice,' he said slowly. He wasn't getting much out of Logan, so James decided to move onto the next kid. 'Now Kimberly, did your Mommy, um, take good care of you where you lived?'

'Yeah! We had so much fun. Daddy would take Logan and me on his back and we'd pretend to be air planes,' she sighed, slouching at the memory that she knew was gone. Macey still smiled a genuine smile when she realized that her kids could be so defensive without even knowing it.

'And they weren't the only things that flew. Dylan and I would show the kids butterflies all the time on the beach. Kim and Logan would try to catch them, and then after watching them, they'd let them go and watch them fly into the sunset. Then we would all relax on the beach until nightfall, and we'd try to count the stars,' Macey smiled dreamily, remembering the cute moments they had all shared.

She looked over at James, curious as to how his expression had changed. His eyes seemed distant, as if he was hoping for something that he had been deprived of. But James didn't let that side show on camera. 'We're not getting much information here,' he sighed, clearly referring to hidden secrets or what not.' Why don't we bring out the helmets?' he said. Macey's face paled. 'The helmets' didn't sound very appealing. They probably did something wacky; another invention of the BCs.

'What do they do?' Macey asked, speaking her mind.

'Oh, not too much. They'll extract most memories from you and your kids' mind, and we'll replay them for our audience before placing them back inside your head.'

'B-but, we will get them back, right?' she asked, not wanting to let go of the moments she feared were gone forever.

'Sure, sure,' James said, not really looking sure at all. Still, he seemed to read Macey's mind. 'Fine, tell you what. We'll use the memory readers. Those will play it all right out of your head. No need to extract them. It's going to hurt a little bit, but the memories will be in your head for you to keep.'

'I think I'll go with the second option,' Macey exhaled, not feeling like she had a choice.

'Alright,' James smiled into his camera again. 'Bring out

the memory readers.' A tiny woman came running out of the backstage door rolling three things that looked like dryer chairs at a hair salon. They were black and leathery, with a strange, white semi-sphere attached on top. 'Please take a seat on one of these chairs,' James said, gesturing in the chairs' general direction. Macey went to choose a seat first, trying to be a leader for her kids, and wanting to portray a confident character for the BCs of the world. She picked the left most chair, Logan chose the center, and Kimberly filled in the chair on the right.

As the third chair detected weight, all three semi-spheres lowered onto their heads, covering their eyes completely. Macey could hear Logan and Kimberly fussing, but it was no use. They couldn't move.

What happened next was a blur. It was all just a jumble of emotional sounds as Macey and her kids listened to their memories being played out for the world. All the time, a small headache was stirring in Macey's mind, growing more painful by the minute. It felt like an eternity before it was all over, and Macey was sure the *Griffin Show* had even run out of airing time.

'Well, how about that, folks?' James asked when the three Memory Readers were lifted. He seemed in pain that he had spent so much money advertising this show, only to be proven wrong. There were no dirty secrets to show. *If I were him, I'd actually plan out my shows*, Macey thought. But at the same time, James seemed touched by the memories he could never live.

'Maybe life as a human isn't so bad,' James sighed, deciding that it wasn't too late to change his show's point. 'I just proved it to you,' he added with a smile to the camera, as if that was his intention all the time. Macey felt like punching James in the face, but she held herself back when she realized that he did help Macey's social life on Earth. Unintentional help, but it was still help.

'Yes, you're right,' Macey looked down at her lap, and then back up with a smile. 'We humans have something called emotion,' she said sarcastically. 'It allows us to create memories that we'll cherish, and make mistakes that we'll learn from.'

Logan and Kimberly simply nodded, staring with glazed eyes at James. Macey was sure they were the only kids to ever live through this situation: being half human, half BC. But, who knew, maybe she was wrong.

∾

'I understand, but I insist that you let me in,' said James Griffin, standing outside the Presidential Palace. Hosting his show had changed his point of view on humans, and he had arranged a meeting with the President beforehand. 'I have discussed this with the President. Please let me in,' he insisted again. The security guard was arguing that there was no way the President would change his mind on such a large matter.

'Fine,' the guard gave in. 'But only because he talked to you about it.'

'Thank you,' James sighed in relief.

'Whatever,' the guard mumbled, moving out of the way and letting James into the Presidential Palace. James smiled with content. He made his way to the front desk lady and informed her on his meetings and arrangements.

'And what time, exactly, will you be starting this meeting?' the front desk lady asked. With a glance at his watch, James realized only a slim three minutes remained before his huge presentation.

'Not too long until it starts,' he said quickly. 'Where can I find the conference room? I need to set up.' The lady smiled.

'Third floor, second door on the right,' she said.

'Thanks,' James said, but he was already dashing towards the elevator. Once he had reached the conference room, James began turning on the projector and loading his slide show presentation. 'Three minutes, three minutes, three minutes,' he rushed himself. Finally, the projector was hooked up, and his presentation was loaded. 'In 10, 9, 8, 7, 6, 5...'

'Sorry I'm early,' a deep voice boomed as somebody kicked the door opened. A large, half Northern, half LeRoyale looking BC stood at the entrance. He was surrounded by two even larger security guards.

'Oh, why, hello, Mr President,' James rushed through his greeting, eager to finish his presentation before his two hours of time ran out. 'Now if you'll please take a seat and we can get started,' he said with a smile.

'Um, sure,' the President wasn't used to being pushed around by the average BC. 'Now, you have two hours to blow my mind away about letting humans live among us,' he smiled, sarcasm reflecting his statement from every level. Ignoring the President's insulting remark, James introduced his argument.

'Many may choose to differ, but let me explain why a human life...is the way of life.' With a great introduction, James went through his presentation without being interrupted once.

After a quick ninety minutes, only half an hour remained in the two's meeting time. 'Now, you may ask questions.' James concluded his presentation. He sucked in a breath and held it there. He decided he'd breathe it in just to let it go.

'Wonderful ideas you've shown me, James,' nodded the President.' Just one problem.'

'Oh? What's that?' James said, his face falling.

'I hate it. There's no way I'm letting humans share our world. They're so...inadequate. Dainty little thoughts go on in their minds, nothing else,' the President said, his face scrunching up. James's heart raced with bit of resolve.

'N-no! You're wrong. Humans have the ideal life, no unnecessary worries drown their thought flow...and...and humans have something we don't have,' James remembered quickly. The President scoffed, already standing up.

'What's that?' he asked, not expecting a satisfactory answer. But James was serious.

'Immunity.' James didn't need a mind reader to know he had captured the President's attention. The President turned, showing only the right side of his face.

'Continue,' he said in a monotone.

'Kimberly and Logan are the perfect example of why we need to breed with humans for a perfect combination. Smarts, emotion, and immunity. We have everything they don't have; they have everything we don't have. Why not merge?' James said with renewed confidence.

'I think I understand your point. But I'm still not completely agreeing. Tell you what. I'll organise a debate, right here in the

Presidential Palace. Majority wins,' the President finally agreed.

'Sounds fair to me,' smiled James.

'Okay. The debate will be held here in three weeks. Thank you for meeting me today, James,' the President reached over to shake James's hand.

'The pleasure's mine,' he replied. That was the last conversation they exchanged before life as they knew it changed.

∿

Three weeks later, Leslie and Tim sat in front of their broadcast holographic center, completely bored. Tim was able to figure out how to hook up the center in their apartment, and both of them were waiting for something about humans to pop up.

'Nothing's on this channel,' Tim sighed. 'Tune into Channel 56, they do a news broadcast at 7 p.m. every day,' he added.

'Tim, it's only 6:30,' Leslie exhaled. 'We have to find something to entertain us till then.'

'Oh, I know. Channel 37 is probably broadcasting something right now,' Tim said, sounding unsure, but hopeful.

'Fine,' Leslie said, flipping channels.

'And that is the reason I believe humans should live among us,' a man said, standing on a podium that had the emblem of the Presidential Palace on it.

'Oh my god,' Leslie said.

'What?' Tim asked.

'That's the same man from, the…the *Griffin Show*! The guy that interviewed Macey! Remember? By the end of the show, he was convinced humans should live on Earth. I guess he took the matter to the President, because now he's up there, on that podium, leading a debate. Tim, this is amazing! Macey could be changing our futures,' Leslie breathed in heavily after zooming through all that in one breath. All Tim did was arch an eyebrow.

'Yeah,' he said, clearly less excited.

'Tim, I don't think you understand,' Leslie said slowly. 'If James Griffin wins this debate, we can live on Earth without danger. We can combine worlds with the BCs. Tim, this is amazing. Life as we know it is changing.'

Tim nodded his head, information sinking in. 'You're right,' Tim said. 'Macey's doing a phenomenal job is worrying me, as well,' he added sarcastically.

'Don't worry, we'll see her soon if this debate is successful. Let's just...pray for the best.'

'Excellent speech, Mr Griffin,' the President came onto the screen. 'Now, we see our opposition.' Another man joined the president on stage, and began shooting out reasons why humans should stay away from Earth.

'Wait a second,' Tim said. 'L-look at the audience.' Leslie didn't see anything out of the ordinary.

'What?' she asked, exasperated.

'Look! Front row, right corner. It's...it's Macey. She's right there,' Tim said, his eyes opening wide.

'No way,' Leslie said, sitting up straighter. 'What the heck is she doing there?'

'Well, she kind of is the big thing. The spark of the whole debate,' Tim admitted to himself. Leslie made a face.

'She's going to get beaten up by the opposing team,' she whined.

'It's going to be okay. Like you said, let's pray for the best. Macey's going to be fine,' he added. Suddenly, somebody on the screen shouted out loud.

'Everybody! Hasn't it come to your attention yet? The human on the *Griffin Show* is the same human we captured two years ago! She'd escaped and now she's back. Arrest her immediately! We should not even be discussing this case. Humans make me sick,' he hollered, waving a picture of Macey which had been taken two years ago. It was the picture that had been used on all of her 'wanted' pictures after she had escaped. Eventually, the pictures had been taken down; the BCs were beginning to see that she probably wasn't coming back. But they were wrong.

A mumble rippled through the crowd, uneasiness and panic becoming visible in the audience members' faces. 'That man is right!' a woman shouted. 'We are unsafe here!' she added. As expected, this angered James. He rose to protest.

'Have you not seen enough evidence? We are the monsters in this situation. Earth was meant for humans. They made our life possible. How do we thank them? By driving them off the face of our—I mean their—planet. They return, to see their home. We respond by capturing the captain's daughter. At least one other BC saw the monster in us, and helped her escape. Now, we're holding her hostage...again? I think you BCs don't realize how heartless you all really are,' James shot.

Another wave went through the crowd, and the positive remark sent renewed hope in Tim and Leslie's direction. Still, the audience seemed unsure.

'These humans also ruined us. If it wasn't for them, we'd never have to go through the physical labour we went through. Getting rid of them was the best decision we've ever made! They were using us like slaves. We're not their little puppets. They made us this way, we have minds of our own, too,' the first man cried.

'Attention!' shouted the President, wanting to keep order in the room. 'Every body will get a chance to state his/her opinion. This matter will be resolved through the age old trusted method of voting! Please, everybody, take one ballot and cast your vote. Results will be counted and revealed in precisely two hours. Until then, no recounts may be demanded. Thank you,' the President stepped off the podium. Almost as if on cue, chaos erupted everywhere. People raided the ballot table as if it was a refreshment stand after a week of fasting. The President and James were shouting one thing, while the crowd was shouting another.

Even in the hologram, you could see that people were being shoved and stepped on; it was almost guaranteed somebody would emerge hurt. Cries of pain sounded everywhere, but no sources could be found. Volunteers moved away from behind counters and tried helping people by passing out ballots to the outskirts of the crowd.

All the time, James was trying to convince all the BCs to vote for and not against. 'Immunity. What does it mean? Can you imagine not having to worry about visiting Forbidden Earth, the most beautiful place on this planet? Can you imagine having colds and coughs be everyday things; nothing to worry about? That's what life would be like if you had a heart and let humans have their home back. It's a win-win situation, really…' he rambled.

After what seemed like an eternity, everybody had filled out a ballot and was seated again. 'Thank you for your… patience,' the President sighed, standing at the podium again. 'Now please excuse us as we tally up the votes. Sorry for any inconvenience, but nobody is permitted to leave until then.' The crowd groaned, but Leslie and Tim sat on the edge of their seats.

'What do you think will happen?' Leslie opened her eyes until they looked like they might pop.

'Honestly, I think that James guy is making a huge impact on our case. Who would've thought that?' Tim replied. Leslie scoffed.

'You heard the guy. All he wants is our immunity,' she snarled. 'He doesn't care about us.'

'Maybe he does. You saw what happened when they played back Macey's memories. 'The guy', as you put him, might actually want our lifestyle,' Tim shrugged. Leslie still didn't seem convinced.

'Bogus,' she tossed her hair back, as if dismissing the case. But Tim wanted to argue more.

'Oh come on, Leslie. You have something to learn from James. Have a heart,' he laughed.

The two had an entertaining argument for nearly an hour, followed by an hour of popcorn, soda, and more laughs. Tim sighed with happiness. He felt it was the happiest he could possibly be with Macey gone.

'Ahh,' he closed his eyes. 'That was fun,' he sighed again, speaking his mind.

'Wait! The tallied ballots! It's been two hours,' Leslie shot up. Tim just lolled his head.

'You go ahead, Leslie. I'm...going...to...sleep...' Tim never finished, he just dropped his head onto the sofa arm-rests. Leslie rolled her eyes in exasperation.

'Come on, Tim!' she urged him. But he had fallen so quickly into deep sleep. So, Leslie switched on the holographic projector for herself. She'd already missed five minutes of the program, but nothing important had been revealed yet.

'Th-thank you James. You may sit down now,' the President commanded. It seemed as if James had started yet another speech on humans. Even Leslie, a human herself, was starting to get annoyed.

'Reveal the results,' she said, clenching her fists. As if the President could hear her, he responded.

'Now for the results!' he blinked, as if determining what he should expect. 'And the final say is...what?' he stopped, obviously not seeing what he was expecting in his result envelope. 'I guess humans can stay on Earth,' he seemed baffled, a little thrown off by his results.

James and Macey could be seen in the audience, mouthing words like 'congratulations' and 'thank you' to each other. Although they were relieved, neither of them could safely say that the worst was over. Neither of them could say the worst had even begun.

∾

19

Revolution

'Thank you, Dylan Brown, for your time spent here at the Northern Earth Medical Center. You are now officially dismissed,' the main nurse smiled.

'Thanks,' Dylan mumbled. 'Now can you please tell me where Macey is?'

'Right,' the nurse said, her face falling as if it was a question she wanted to avoid. 'Macey's secret was discovered. I'm sure I don't have to tell you what that secret was.'

Dylan decided playing dumb would be a waste. Instead, he acted as shocked as he really was. 'What? Wait, is she okay? Where did they take her?'

'Relax,' the nurse sighed, as she began to explain everything, from the *Griffin Show* to the debate. 'She's okay now, and humans will now be permitted in certain areas of Earth,' the nurse finished. Dylan opened his eyes wide, and smiled from ear to ear.

'That's great! I knew my Macey was special enough to start

a revolution. She's the one for me. This is just...wonderful,' he let out a huge breath, heaving his shoulders.

'I'd like to meet your mother. Only a crazy woman could raise a child like you,' the nurse muttered under her breath. Dylan's face fell. Not because his mother had just been referred to as crazy, but because his mother was 'referred to' at all. Dylan had been so busy trying to raise a family of his own, he had forgotten about the family that had raised him.

April probably had hundreds of 'MISSING' signs up everywhere. 'Hey, no hard feelings,' the nurse reassured him, obviously thinking Dylan was upset because she referred to his mother as crazy.

'I know,' Dylan said, looking down. 'I haven't seen her in two years. I really need to go and meet her,' Dylan said, pushing through the main door into the late afternoon sun. He sprinted down the cool city sidewalk, racing towards home at an immeasurable pace. 'April!' he yelled all the way, in case she was roaming downtown instead of sitting at home. 'Mom!' Dylan tried again. Finally he reached his old doorstep. 'Home,' he exhaled. Dylan knew that this was his last hope. If April wasn't at home, only God knew where she was. Finally, Dylan knocked.

He silently thanked the heavens when he heard footsteps. A tear-streaked face opened the door. 'I've told you a million times. I'm not going to offer any money to somebody who's only seen Dylan. I need somebody who knows where...' April stopped short when she looked up. 'Dylan?' she asked. By that point of time, Dylan was about as teary as April.

'Mom!' he hollered, wrapping his strong arms around her

weak body. April took in a deep breath and closed her eyes. She was trying to remember the last time she had held Dylan so close.

'Dylan, I never thought I'd see your face again,' April breathed.

'I'm surprised you didn't have the SWAT team searching for me,' Dylan laughed, making a joke out of the serious situation. April drew back and held Dylan's head in her hands for a few moments.

'Come inside. Tell me everything. I want to know why you left, what happened while you were gone, and what you learned,' April said, turning sharply into the house. 'It's time to start explaining.' Dylan followed April into the kitchen and sat down at the head of the dining table. April sat across from him. 'Spill. Now.' Dylan sighed. He rambled in a monotone about what happened after the history museum exhibit, how he helped Macey escape, how he raised a family, and why he ended up in the hospital. When Dylan was done, he finally looked up into April's eyes.

The green beauties were immeasurably large, filled with all sorts of emotions: fear, worry, love, forgiveness, and anger. All at the same time. 'Oh, sugar,' she sighed, her voice dipped in a light country accent. 'That's horrible,' she breathed, reaching for Dylan's hands. Dylan pulled back.

'Mom, right now's not the time. Just because I came back, doesn't mean I'm ready to let go of the life I was leading.' April was taken aback.

'But…that life was horrible,' she whispered, looking down and eying Dylan through her eyelashes.

'No, it wasn't. I want to go back. You were so intent on seeing Macey at the History Museum. I went above and beyond; I fell in love with her. I admit it; you were right when you told me that night at the museum would change my life. Now why are you rejecting Macey?' Dylan snapped. On the outside, he was frustrated, but his eyes implied the fact that he was being incredibly apprehensive.

'No, Dylan,' April whined. 'Stop fighting. You just got back from the hospital. I don't want to fight with you.'

'Fine, then. But you must admit one thing,' Dylan held his chin up. 'You're utterly curious as to with whom I've been spending the past few years of my life.'

April stared at him blankly. 'No, I'm not,' she said, matter-of-factly. Dylan shot her an intimidating glare, informing her that he wanted the truth.

'Well,' he dragged. 'I think it'd be reasonable for the two of you to meet up. Macey's the funniest, smartest, most beautiful woman you'll ever meet.' April groaned.

'Dylan, you know how dangerous it is for a BC to visit Forbidden Earth. You even experienced the pain. Yet, you still refuse to stay safe,' she said. 'You're unbelievable.'

'Mom, please,' Dylan scoffed. 'I know you're curious. You've been curious about everything that goes on in my life from the day you adopted me.'

'Right,' April said, tensing up when she heard the word 'adopted' slip out of Dylan's mouth. If Dylan noticed the uneasiness that had formed in April, he definitely didn't show it.

'What do you say?' Dylan rolled his eyes, clearly annoyed at April's avoidance of his question.

'Please Dylan, don't do this to me,' April cried, a tear rolling down her cheek at the thought of losing Dylan again.

'I'm sorry Mom. But I have to. This is my life now. You can join me, or you can sit here and watch me walk out of the door. Don't get me wrong; I love you so much. But I think I'm old enough to live my own life now.' Dylan, who was convinced April wasn't ready to visit Forbidden Earth, stood up to show that he wasn't joking. He exited the kitchen and entered the main hall. But before leaving through the door, Dylan hesitated. The whole I'm-leaving act was just an action to leave April with no choice.

But if April wasn't responding, Dylan didn't know what he'd do. To cover up his secret, Dylan quickly opened the door and slammed it shut again, without ever leaving the house. Finally, he heard the sound of feet softly padding to the main door.

'Dylan, wait!' April howled, not aware Dylan hadn't ditched the house yet.

'Mom, I'm right here,' Dylan said softly, when April came into sight. April's formerly perfect eyeliner appeared to be getting a hint of smudge and wetness.

'Dylan, let's go,' April said, sniffing. Now that Dylan had gotten what he wanted, he wasn't so sure if it was a good idea after all.

'But Mom, you just said,' Dylan started.

'Don't question me; I said let's go,' April said. Dylan, delighted, followed April through the front door. 'Oh wait,' April said, stopping. 'You took my teleporter while you were gone, didn't you?' April sighed.

Dylan smiled and nodded sheepishly. Suddenly, he perked up just a hair. 'Well, I know where it is. Macey, Logan, Kimberly, Emma, and I used your teleporter to get to the hospital when Macey called the Northern Earth Medical Center. It's probably still in a reserved parking spot there.' April rolled her eyes.

'That's just something you would do, Dylan,' April said, placing her hands on her hips. 'Well, come on. We'll run over to the hospital, pick up the teleporter, and then zoom back to Forbidden Earth.' Dylan was surprised by April's sudden enthusiasm.

'Sure thing, Mom. Here, let me grab your shoes for you,' Dylan said, in an attempt to be helpful.

'Dylan, Dylan, silly Dylan,' April shook her head. 'You still don't understand, do you? I use high heels to go everywhere. Looking good isn't high-maintenance. It's easy. Just slip on a pair of April's shoes,' she laughed. Dylan rolled his eyes. But suddenly, a thought occurred to him.

'I don't even know where Macey is,' he said with disbelief. 'Why are we even going to Forbidden Earth? For all we know, Macey could still be here, in Northern Earth. The last I heard of her was during the debate, when her side won. When the *Griffin Show* host convinced us to keep humans on Earth. Where could she even be?'

April stared at Dylan blankly, like he was missing something huge. 'Dylan. Don't act stupid. What do you do when you're searching for a famous person's whereabouts?' Dylan pondered her point for a moment.

'Duh. The news.' Dylan felt moronic as he switched the holographic projector on. The same reporters that were fussing them if they can't find their family?'

'I'm sure Macey watched the news while you were in the hospital. After all, she was the spotlight of every report,' April said, matter-of-factly. Dylan agreed with a nod of his head. 'They must've uncovered the secret hall they've been staying in. She's probably already found her friends and family.'

'You're probably right,' Dylan said, walking out of the spaceship and circling it; he was trying to find the secret entrance that led to Macey's temporary home. All the time, he was conversing with his mom.

'How do you think they're going to establish a safe community for humans? Are the BCs going to help out? Is it going to be a community service kind of thing? What'll happen if some BCs are still very against the idea of breeding with humans?' Dylan would ask all sorts of questions, for he was not able to imagine what such a different world would be like.

April stayed silent all the time, as if she was absorbing the questions through her skin, but they never made it to her mind. 'Found it,' April mumbled softly, kicking loose a rusty piece of metal on the spaceship to reveal a steep drop into something that seemed like a hallway.

'That's great!' Dylan said, trying to be high-spirited. Even though April was the one who found the passage, Dylan was the one to jump through it first. He didn't wait for April though; instead he continued down the corridor.

'Great,' April sighed, sarcasm reflecting off her voice. 'How do we know which room's Macey's?' Dylan smirked.

'Watch this.' Dylan cupped his hands around his mouth and began to shout. 'Logan! Kimberly! Did you miss Daddy?'

about the huge virus attack years ago stood in the spotlight again; this time with smiles plastered across their cheesy faces.

'The results have been announced!' famous reporter, Amy Bell screeched. 'None of us were expecting this, but Macey Johnson, a visitor from space, has started a revolution on Earth! Humans will now be tolerated on Earth. However, many of them will stay in Forbidden Earth, for they have no risk of getting hurt there...' Dylan paced back in forth in front of the hologram. Growing impatient, he started shouting.

'Tell us where the girl is,' he demanded. As if the hologram was a magic mirror, it answered Dylan's question immediately.

'This legendary Macey Johnson has been sent back to Forbidden Earth, for it is there where her family's spaceship supposedly 'crashed'. However, after closer investigation, the Police Department discovered the accident was merely a prank. Before the debate, this kind of behaviour would lead to serious punishment. Luckily for the Johnsons, a law has just recently been passed that humans shall not be chastised unless they have committed a crime. Technically, this feat was not a cri-,' Amy Bell never got to finish. Dylan had shut off the projector already.

'Forbidden Earth! That's where she is! That's incredible news. Her family's there too? This...is absolutely perfect,' Dylan announced. April just smiled in his direction.

'It's good to see you grow up, Dylan. To find your true love before twenty-five? That's amazing,' she joked. Suddenly, Dylan thought of who his real dad might be. He let the thought slip from his mind as he shoved April through the door.

'Come on! We've got places to go and people to see.'

The two of them began jogging down the sidewalk, heading directly for the hospital.

∾

A couple of minutes later, April's teleporter glided onto the sandy shores of Forbidden Earth. Dylan pointed out the home he built a couple yards away. April stayed quiet, in spite of Dylan's explanations. It was as if she was trying to imagine what living in such a place could be like. The only words April bothered to say were warnings like 'Look out for bees' and 'Be careful'. After exploring the beach for a little bit, Dylan dragged April into the forests and started searching for the spaceship landing site.

'It's about five miles east of Lima Lake,' Dylan recalled. April scoffed and made a 'psh' sound with her lips.

'That's no biggie. First of all, we could just use a teleporter to get to Lima Lake. Second, I can already hear the Lima Lake waterfall. That way,' April gestured vaguely in an eastern direction. Dylan rolled his eyes.

'I knew that,' he laughed sarcastically. He bent down to tie is shoe; his laces had untied and were covered in green-brown, tenacious mud. By the time Dylan looked up again, April had zoomed over to a patch of poorly kept redwood trees.

'Dylan!' she hooted over her shoulder. 'Come check it out.' At first Dylan was uncertain; it was unlikely the spaceship was so easy to find. But as Dylan neared the clearing she was peering through, he realized April had found the location he was looking for.

April shushed him.

'Dylan! Don't you know that there are other humans here? Besides your little family? I thought I taught you manners as a child!' April exclaimed. But she hollered no more as soon as she saw a little girl and boy running out from the door at the end of the hall.

'It's okay,' Dylan smiled reassuringly. 'I think they're expecting me.'

'Daddy!' Kimberly dragged, bouncing up to embrace him. Logan stood behind her, waiting for his chance to hug his father.

'Kimberly, Logan, meet your grandmother, Grandma April,' he laughed.

'Don't make me feel old,' April joked. 'I look young enough to be their mother!' April knelt down and held her arms out to Logan, who ran into them gratefully.

'Hi Grandma,' he said, his blond hair rubbing against her chest.

'It's nice to finally get to meet you,' a new voice said. Both Dylan and April looked up.

'Macey!' Dylan exhaled, running over to embrace her. 'Are you okay? What you did to our world was...amazing. You're a celebrity now! Literally!' Macey returned the hug, but only half-heartedly. First, she wanted to meet her mother-in-law.

'Hi. It's nice to see you as well,' April said. She left Logan so she could shake Macey's hand. 'Dylan's told me a lot about you. You really did start a revolution.' April smiled. Dylan and Macey both blushed.

'Why thank you,' Macey gushed. 'Oh, why don't you come inside? You can meet my dad, Tim, and my best friend, Leslie.

In front of him lay a battered, ash covered spaceship. To further their exploration, April and Dylan entered the trashed spaceship and looked around. It was apparent that the whole 'fake explosion' trick had been taken care of, because fake ash had been swept to small corners and old pictures had been hung up at a tacky angle.

'Macey!' Dylan called, remembering what the two of them had come for.

'Dylan. Seriously, haven't you listened to the news lately?' April said, annoyed.

Dylan arched an eyebrow, reminding April that he'd been in the hospital for a while. By her expression, Dylan could tell April wanted to take back her comment.

'Well, right after the debate, Amy Bell told everybody— literally, you couldn't live on this Earth without hearing her yell out her message over and over again, 'It's not technically a crime, but humans have been keeping a secret all along. The whole 'crashed spaceship' act was just a prank,' April said.

'Yeah, yeah I know that part,' Dylan muttered, gesturing for April to continue.

'Well, you don't know the main part of the scandal. Where do you think these humans stayed after their spaceship crashed? No bodies were found.' Dylan remained speechless. April took that as a sign to continue. 'It turns out they've been living underground in these cell-like rooms all this time.'

'Then how does Macey know where to find her family? The news reporter did say she was sent back to Forbidden Earth,' Dylan pointed out. 'Logan and Kimberly—our kids— are probably with her too. What'll happen to the three of

Would you like a cup of coffee?' she added.

'No thanks,' April said. 'I think I'd just like to stay awhile. Get to know my family.' Macey smiled gratefully. Meeting her mother-in-law wasn't nearly as stressful as she thought it would be. As April walked inside, she came face to face with a younger version of herself. 'Hi, I am Leslie. I'm Macey's friend.' April's earlier years, that she had tried so hard to forget, flashed before her eyes. Trying hard to swallow the sudden lump in her throat, April greeted Tim. Tim and Leslie could not understand the sudden transition of April's mood to a solemn one.

Still outside the room, Macey whispered to Dylan 'I'm so glad you could make it. It's fantastic you brought your mom. She really is as pretty as she looked in the pictures,' Macey grinned. Dylan returned her smile with a bright beam, and walked through the door without another word. Macey, Logan, and Kim were only two steps behind.

When Macey joined everybody in the family room, she slowly observed everything that was going on around her. She had expected everybody to be getting along and laughing together, but instead, everybody remained silent. The unfamiliar absence of sound caused distress in all of them, as they all squirmed in their seats.

'What's going on?' Macey inquired, trying to brighten the mood.

'I think the time has come,' April said.

'What are you talking about?' Leslie asked this time. 'I'm sorry; I don't mean to be rude. I'm just utterly confused right now,' she fumbled.

'I agree with Leslie,' Dylan said, his eyebrows scrunching together suspiciously. Tim took a deep breath, but didn't say anything. Even he wanted to hear what came next.

'Kids, I never thought this day would come. The day when I would have to tell you what I'm about to tell you. I imagined we'd live our life like normal humans or BCs. But it's occurred to me that…it's time,' April said, sitting up as straight as possible. She reached over and took Leslie's hand in her own. Leslie was shocked, since she had no connections with April whatsoever. But Leslie knew her manners, and let April hold on.

'Leslie, you're my daughter.' April was dead serious. Despite April's sincerity, Leslie laughed.

'Nice joke, Mrs Brown. Very funny. I think we all fell for it, right guys?' Leslie nodded towards the rest of their party. Everybody laughed nervously.

'Leslie, I'm not joking,' April responded. Suddenly, Dylan cut in.

'Mom. I'm kind of confused here. So you had a real daughter, gave her up, and then adopted a son? That doesn't make any sense.' April sighed.

'I have a lot of explaining to do, don't I?' Everybody nodded, their expressions proving that the question wasn't even worth asking—the answer was obvious.

'April, I'm so very sorry to interrupt you, but please stop joking around.' Tim said calmly.

'But I swear! I'm telling the truth right now! Please, just listen to me.' Tim considered her plea.

'Fine. We'll listen to your story, but if we find out you're playing a prank on us, I'm afraid you won't be welcome in this house again,' Tim stated firmly.

'Agreed,' April nodded, clearly confident that her story was the solid truth. 'Here's basically what happened. In my college years, I fell madly in love with this man named Josh. It was no shock when we eventually got married. We lived happily for two years, but that was until he confessed a secret to me. He was human.' Macey laughed out loud. 'What?' April snapped.

'How in the world would another human be on Earth? I was told I was one of the first to be captured,' Macey pointed out. April, however, was prepared for this question.

'His great grandfather and great grandmother were left behind when the last human spaceship took off of Earth. Desperate to keep the human bloodline alive on Earth, the two gave birth to a daughter and a son, who then crossed, and so on and so forth. Josh didn't have any siblings though, so it became clear to us that he would most likely be the last human on Earth. That's when I offered to help continue his blood line. I'm a BC, I know, but at least our children would be half human. Of course he agreed.' April stopped to see how everybody was reacting. Nobody said a word, so April continued.

'First we gave birth to Dylan,' April gestured in his direction. 'Then, a year later, Leslie came along. Shortly afterwards, though, a virus attack struck Forbidden Earth. Everybody had to get a test done to see if they were contaminated or not. Those who did carry the virus were put immediately to 'sleep'—as they put it. We knew we would have to fake Josh's test, or his secret would be discovered. But the day before the test, I woke up, and he was...gone. He had stopped breathing. He killed himself to save me.' Everybody gave out a short 'aww'.

'It occurred to the humans a little too late,' April said bitterly. 'But they did come back for Josh's family. To see if they were still here. Of course, I couldn't say I had two of his children. So instead, I decided to hide Leslie on the spaceship before they took off. I guess that's where Tim found you,' she said to Leslie.

'Why get rid of me? Was I your least-liked child?' Leslie said, offended.

'No! Nothing like that. You're beautiful, Leslie. It's just that you were more on the human side than the BC side, and Dylan the opposite. It'd be easier to keep Dylan in a world of BCs, you see?' April answered quickly, taking Leslie's hand in her own. Leslie nodded. 'Also, you look just like your father. When I looked at your face, it brought me great grief. I saw him in you. I decided it was time to let go and move on. I told Dylan he was adopted and that I didn't know anything about his past just so that he wouldn't question his origin. As for you, Leslie, you were too young to remember any of this, so of course, your past remained a mystery for you. So, you grew up as a human, Dylan as a BC. But I guess the event of you two finding each other was meant to be, because look here now. It's kind of like a family reunion, when you think about it.'

Tim's jaw dropped. 'April, this just seems so...fake.' April's face fell.

'You don't believe me? I'll do anything. Heck, I'll even

purchase a genetic test if you want me to!' she responded. Tim shook his head.

'It's just really hard, accepting this so-called reality,' Tim said in disbelief.

'Look on the bright side. It's still okay if this story gets to the press, because humans are allowed on Earth now,' April winked. Macey's face brightened.

'Finally, all of our secrets are being cleansed out of our souls. We're starting on a fresh slate,' she fluttered happily. Tim smiled at the sight of Macey's happiness.

'You know what, April? I actually think it'd be a great idea to get this story published. This is kind of like the ending. The event that ties all loose ends together,' Tim said, an image of a magazine with all their names on the cover popping into his mind. April smiled back gratefully.

'I'm so glad we could get this cleared up. Now, if you'll excuse me, I have a news station to call,' April laughed, whipping out her cell phone. It felt as if a layer of tension had been stripped off their shoulders, lightening the burden that they had carried through out.

∾

20

---⊶⊷⊶---

Unexpected Results

For the next week, Mrs Anderson and her two kids were asked to find a different room, for Dylan and April moved in with Tim, Leslie, Macey, and Macey's kids. April, as she had promised, got the press to publish her appalling story.

'Come on, come on!' Dylan summoned everybody to the couches in front of the projector. 'Amy Bell's about to do a cover report on our story!' Leslie and Macey squealed, going back to how they used to be before Macey was kidnapped. Logan and Kimberly entertained themselves by making forts out of pillows and bed sheets, and April had joined Tim for a good chat in the kitchen. But all of them came together to watch their faces on the broadcast.

'Okay! News at seven starts...now!' Dylan exclaimed, switching the hologram set on. Dramatic music played as the blue and silver symbol for the news station appeared, accompanied with high-tech graphics. News reporter Amy Bell showed up on the screen, her shoulder-length brown hair pulled back with a blue headband.

'Lately, many interesting events have been occurring in Northern Earth. But now, the biggest shocker of them all has been revealed to us. Can it be that Macey's best friend—Leslie Stevens, is related to the well known BC—Dylan Brown? It has to be true! We have the proof right here, straight from the witnesses themselves...'

'Sorry to interrupt you, Amy. But we have bigger news,' a famous reporter named Jared Smith suddenly took Amy's place on the big screen.

'No problem,' Amy said. But it was very apparent that Amy didn't like being interrupted at all.

'We have just received news from the Presidential Palace. Apparently, hundreds of cases were recently filed reporting that more half-human, half-BCs are scattered around Earth. How these people could keep such a big secret is still unknown, but the idea is absolutely shocking. The President is wondering just how much he really knows about the world he's running. What other secrets are yet to be discovered? What else has been hidden in this world?'

∾

Back in the Presidential Palace, chaos had erupted everywhere. Officials were wondering how much longer until Earth was under humans' control again. Citizens were wondering how the President was handling things. As for the President...he was growing impatient with everything.

New secrets were being uncovered, decoded, and revealed

constantly. How much did the BCs really know about their world? And what lay in their future? It was all a mystery.

But that's a whole other story.

॰∾